Finding Christmas

a Blue Harbor novel

OLIVIA MILES

Rosewood Press

ALSO BY OLIVIA MILES

Blue Harbor Series
A Place for Us
Second Chance Summer
Because of You
Small Town Christmas
Return to Me
Then Comes Love

Stand-Alone Titles
Summer's End
Meet Me at Sunset
This Christmas

Oyster Bay Series
Feels Like Home
Along Came You
Maybe This Time
This Thing Called Love
Those Summer Nights
Christmas at the Cottage
Still the One
One Fine Day
Had to Be You

Misty Point Series
One Week to the Wedding
The Winter Wedding Plan

Sweeter in the City Series
Sweeter in the Summer
Sweeter Than Sunshine
No Sweeter Love
One Sweet Christmas

Briar Creek Series
Mistletoe on Main Street
A Match Made on Main Street
Hope Springs on Main Street
Love Blooms on Main Street
Christmas Comes to Main Street

Harlequin Special Edition
'Twas the Week Before Christmas
Recipe for Romance

Copyright © 2021 by Megan Leavell
ISBN 978-1-7346208-8-7

All rights reserved. No part of this publication may be reproduced, distributed or transmitted in any form or by any means, without prior written permission.

Publisher's Note: This is a work of fiction. Names, characters, places, and incidents are a product of the author's imagination. Locales and public names are sometimes used for atmospheric purposes. Any resemblance to actual people, living or dead, or to businesses, companies, events, institutions, or locales is completely coincidental.

Finding Christmas

1

There was no better month in Blue Harbor than December, at least to Jenna Conway. The snow was fresh, the air was crisp, and Christmas decorations were everywhere she turned. Store windows had traded colorful fall leaves for paper snowflakes, lampposts were wrapped in garland secured with bright-red velvet bows, and people were in good spirits all around, lifted by the miniature lights that sparkled and shone from dusk until dawn.

And of course, as if the cookies and presents and hot chocolate weren't enough, December was a time for Jenna's favorite thing: Christmas carols.

A cold gust of wind forced Jenna to pause and wrap her red cashmere scarf tighter around her neck before she continued along Main Street, careful not to slip on any icy patches that hadn't yet been salted because the only thing that could ruin the holidays for her was a sprained wrist. She couldn't play the piano without the use of both her hands, and, reminding herself of this, she slowed her pace. She arrived at Buttercream Bakery shivering but smiling a few minutes later, appreciating the aroma of roasting coffee and warm gingerbread.

"It smells like the North Pole in here," she told her cousin Maddie as she approached the counter. In true Blue Harbor fashion, Maddie had swapped her usual apron for one that was red-and-white-striped, and the long glass display case was draped in garland and twinkling lights.

"It must be the candy cane hot cocoa muffins," Maddie pointed to a basket of oversized muffins topped with a pink peppermint crumble.

Jenna's stomach grumbled. She'd been so busy prepping last-minute ideas for this year's Christmas pageant that she hadn't found time to eat breakfast, and she probably wouldn't if she wanted to get to the school in time for her planning meeting.

"Muffins? Or cupcakes?" Jenna grinned.

Maddie laughed. "Anything goes when it comes to the holidays, even candy with your breakfast." She pulled a bakery box tied with a red ribbon from behind the counter and slid it across the wooden surface to Jenna. "Here's your order. A dozen of my holiday shortbread cookies. A baker's dozen, that is."

Jenna lifted the box carefully, resisting the urge to pop the lid and sneak an early taste. Maddie's shortbread was buttery and rich with just the right amount of sweetness. She'd been perfecting the recipe for years before opening this establishment, and they were a crowd-pleaser at their annual cookie swap party.

"I'm sure that Suzanne will be thrilled," she said, thinking of how the school's principal was a regular customer here. "I have a few suggestions for this year's pageant and these should help sweeten the deal, so to speak."

Jenna had been thinking about it for months, ever since the air turned crisp and the leaves began to fall and Christmas crept into her mind. The pageant was something that she'd participated in for the past several years, accompanying the children on the piano and helping the music teacher with the weekly rehearsals. It was a fairly standard event, with the same grades performing the same songs, and with Mr. Pritchard in his final year at the school, she doubted he had much energy to shake things up, even though he was always delighted to hear her ideas. This year, Jenna hoped to make things a little different, a little more special, to honor the teacher who had taught her so much.

"I'm sure she'll love whatever you have to share," Maddie reassured her.

Jenna, however, wasn't so sure. "Suzanne loves traditions nearly as much as Cora," Jenna said, referring to Maddie's sister who owned the town's holiday shop.

Maddie raised her eyebrows. The entire town knew how wedded Cora was to her Christmas traditions, but the family members knew best. For years, no one had dared to so much as disrupt the order of the ornament hanging, until recently when so many of Jenna's cousins had found relationships. Her sisters too, Jenna thought, and mentally added Brooke's husband and Gabby's boyfriend to her gift list.

"Cora managed to open her mind to new ideas last year and look how that turned out! She's already talking about all the new activities she plans to do with that boyfriend of hers and his sweet little girl," Maddie said. "I'm sure that Suzanne will do the same, especially coming from the musical expert!"

Jenna's cheeks burned despite the chill that still clung to her coat. "I'm just a piano teacher."

"You also play at weddings!" Maddie scolded, but her eyes were bright. "And heading up the Christmas choir is no small feat!"

It was true, all true, but there was a part of Jenna that always felt like she hadn't lived up to her potential, or had at least come up short. Her heart swelled with pride when she taught a little girl how to play her favorite song, or when the entire town came out to gather at the town square for the annual tree lighting, where she was often asked to accompany everyone with classic carols. But there was always a nagging thought of what could have been, if…

She stopped herself there. No sense thinking of what might have been. She was a piano teacher, a local accompanist, a substitute music teacher at the school, and today she had an important meeting and one that she had been looking forward to all week.

"I should run." Jenna was just as desperate to change the topic as she was to pitch her idea to Suzanne. "Will I see you at the tree lighting on Friday?"

Maddie nodded. "Wouldn't miss it."

No, Maddie would never skip a Blue Harbor tradition, and neither would anyone else in Jenna's family. The Conways were deeply rooted in this town, and expanding by the day with so many of her cousins and sisters now coupled off or, in her cousin Britt's case, even engaged. It was the bright side to living here in her hometown—Jenna was surrounded by the people who knew and loved her best, and others who were happy to support her musical endeavors. If she'd been accepted to that music conservatory all those years ago, she could be living a different life in a major city, or touring with an orchestra. And a different life wasn't necessarily a better one. Or so she told herself on the days when the insecurities still reared, and the memory of rejection stung.

She had a family she loved and a job that satisfied her. And it was Christmas. No time to be harping on old hurts.

Jenna scooted out of line to let the next person move up to the counter. The walk to the school was short, and Jenna chose the scenic path, hugging the lakeshore until she cut up to Main Street near the harbor, and then hurried up the steps to the double doors of the very school she'd once attended.

She waved to Lauren Mackenzie at the front desk as she approached. "I'm here for the pageant meeting."

Lauren gave a funny expression and then said, "I think Mr. Pritchard is expecting you."

"Oh, I'm sure he's positively bouncing in his chair by now!" Jenna laughed. Mr. Pritchard loved the concert as much as she did, and his enthusiasm was contagious, drawing her in at a young age.

Lauren chewed her lip as if she had something more to say, but just then a little boy came in through the door, sniffling and crying about a lost lunch box, and that was Jenna's cue to exit. Besides, she didn't want to keep Mr. Pritchard waiting—they likely had a limited window before his next class.

With a smile, Jenna followed the familiar halls to Mr. Pritchard's room and stood in the open doorway, where another man was already perched on a student desk, his back to Jenna, deep in conversation. Hesitantly, Jenna transferred her box of cookies to one hand and rapped her knuckles against the door with the other, drawing the attention of sweet Mr. Pritchard and a man whom Jenna had never seen before in town.

A rather good-looking man.

"Jenna!" Mr. Pritchard smiled as he stood and crossed the room to clasp her hand in both of his. His watery blue eyes were bright behind his tortoise-shell glasses. "So good to see you, dear."

"And you too, Mr. Pritchard! I always look forward to this meeting. Is Suzanne joining us?"

Mr. Pritchard exchanged a glance with the other man, who had slid off the desk to walk toward her, extending a hand. "I'm Principal Dunne. I'm going to be filling in for Suzanne for the rest of the school year."

Jenna was barely able to hide her shock as she shook the man's hand, but now she studied him a little more closely, liking what she saw. Medium-brown hair with a side part, warm eyes to match, and a smile that was pleasant and carefree.

"Is everything okay with Suzanne?" She couldn't help but worry. When Suzanne had set up this meeting two weeks ago, she hadn't indicated that she wouldn't be attending it.

"She had to head down to Florida for an undetermined amount of time to tend to her mother," Mr. Pritchard explained. "It was sudden and she was unsure as to when she would be back, so the board thought it made sense for Mr. Dunne—I mean, Principal Dunne—to fill in for the remainder of the year."

Jenna nodded, giving the handsome new principal a little smile. "I see, well, it's a pleasure to meet you. I have so many ideas for this year's pageant—"

Mr. Dunne held up a hand. Mr. Pritchard swallowed hard and muttered something about needing to run to class, even though they were standing in his classroom. The very piano she often played sat in the corner near the window, next to a pile of plastic recorders for the younger students.

"I'm afraid we won't be needing your services at the pageant this year," Mr. Dunne said.

Jenna stared at him, aware that he had her at more than one advantage. Not only did she have no idea she wouldn't be meeting with Suzanne, but she was also standing in her coat and scarf, at a meeting that probably should have been canceled.

She blinked hard as her heart began to pound, trying to understand what he was implying. "Did you…find another piano player?"

She hadn't met any competition in the area in all the years that she'd been playing professionally, but perhaps she had been naïve, or just lucky. Perhaps this Mr. Dunne knew another piano player. A better piano player. Perhaps, he was married to one.

"There won't be a Christmas pageant this year," Mr. Dunne replied.

That took a moment to sink in. When Jenna realized from his deadpan expression that he was, in fact, serious, she managed to say, "No pageant?"

"The kids will do a little something for their parents during the class holiday parties instead. It makes sense, and it's budget-friendly, and with the changes going on around here, it felt like a happy compromise."

A happy compromise? There was nothing happy about the thought of the pageant being canceled! What about the costumes, the candles, the music? And what changes was he referring to, other than canceling a beloved community event?

"But...who will accompany them?" She'd gladly volunteer her services.

"Oh, digital accompaniment," he assured her with a strange smile.

Jenna stared at him, resisting the urge to laugh out loud at such a horrible idea. "Digital accompaniment," she clarified slowly.

He nodded. "The arts haven't been well funded in recent years and some cuts are needed—"

Now it was her turn to hold up a hand. "I'm happy to volunteer my services if cost is the issue. I've put a lot of thought into this production and it's, well, a tradition."

Surely, he could understand the value of a Christmas tradition!

"I appreciate that, Jenna, but the decision has already been made and the kids seem quite excited about it. Besides, the individual classrooms don't have a piano and this will allow the teachers to get creative. From what I understand, the holiday pageant has become a little stale in recent years."

Jenna opened her mouth and then closed it. If by stale he meant that the kindergarteners wore reindeer costumes and the first graders were snowmen and every child looked forward to the next year when they'd move up to the next costume, and several parents told Jenna they made ornaments out of the photos from each year, so they could always look back on the time their child was an elf in third grade and a nutcracker in ninth, then yes, the pageant was stale.

A bell rang and Mr. Dunne checked his watch. "I'm afraid I'm due back in my office for a meeting. Thank you for coming in, Jenna. I'm sorry I don't have better news. It's nothing personal, I can assure you."

Oh, but he was wrong about that. This was personal. Deeply personal, and deeply disappointing too.

Jenna swallowed the lump in her throat and nodded her head to show that she understood, even though she didn't agree with it. Still, she couldn't walk away without trying.

"This is Mr. Pritchard's last year at the school," she pointed out, but the new principal just nodded. She took a breath and continued. "I think he would like to have one last pageant." More like he deserved to have one last pageant, and she hoped to give him a special finale this year, one that would involve the entire audience, joining in song, honoring the man who had given so much to their children, and, in some of their cases, to them.

Mr. Dunne opened his mouth and closed it again as if he had changed his mind about how to respond. "All good things must come to an end at some point, as the saying goes."

Jenna swallowed hard, wondering just what her beloved music teacher thought of this sudden change. She intended to seek him out as soon as possible and offer him a few words of comfort. But first, she intended to fight on his behalf.

With one hand holding the bakery box, she attempted to fish her notes from her tote with the other. "I have some great ideas—"

But Mr. Dunne was already leading her to the door. "I'm sure this is something that Suzanne can discuss with you in more depth."

But not with him. Not with this brisk, no-nonsense Principal Dunne, who had made it very clear that he could not be persuaded. Jenna's spirits sank further.

"It's just that it's a Christmas tradition..." She stopped walking, forcing him to look at her properly.

"Thank you for coming in," he replied. "Now, if you'll excuse me."

He gave a tight smile before disappearing into the hallway, leaving Jenna alone in the room where her love for music had first been born, clutching a box of Christmas cookies that she hadn't even been given the chance to share.

So much for starting the season on a high note.

*

Harbor Holidays was by far the most festive shop in all of Blue Harbor, tucked at the end of Main Street in an old Victorian home that sat next door to Bart's tree lot. By the time Jenna arrived, she had already eaten three of the cookies in her box and her cousin Cora was quick to notice.

"Not a baker's dozen from what I see," she tsked, selecting one from the top and giving Jenna a little grin.

"You counted?" Jenna reached for another while her cousin prepared them each a mug of hot chocolate. The shop hadn't opened yet for the day, but she'd come in through Cora's private entrance at the back of the building, directly into the kitchen that was closed off to the shop rooms.

"No. I can see the crumbs all over your scarf." Cora laughed and handed her a candy-cane striped napkin from the center of her table.

Like the meandering rooms that comprised her store, Cora's quarters were overflowing with holiday-themed items, from the red kettle on the stove to the Mr. and Mrs. Clause potholders that hung from the oven handle.

"I just can't believe that this man would waltz into town and change everything! Suzanne hasn't even been gone two weeks. And it's Christmas. It's tradition for me to accompany the kids. It's tradition for them to have a show for their parents! The senior class will never have an opportunity to ring the silver bells for their final song! That's a rite of passage."

Cora gave an understanding cluck as she sat down with their mugs. "This setback might give you a chance to explore some new traditions. That's what happened to me last Christmas when my sisters all decided to make their own plans. I ended up finding a few of my own and new people to share them with, too."

She gave a wistful smile at the mention of her boyfriend and his sweet little girl, Georgie, who had come into Cora's life last holiday season.

But Jenna wasn't convinced. "My music is the most important thing in my life, and Christmas has always been my favorite time to share what I love with everyone."

"Sadly, not everyone loves the holiday as we do," Cora said, shaking her head. She added a few more marshmallows to Jenna's reindeer-shaped mug. "But at what other time of the year can you have hot chocolate and cookies for breakfast and not feel remotely guilty?"

That managed to pull a smile from Jenna. She knew that Cora could.

"You're right, I suppose. There's a lot to look forward to, and next year Suzanne will be back." Jenna hoped so, at least. She turned the mug in her hands. "The new principal implied that there were budget issues and lots of changes going on in the school."

"Maybe he was referring to Suzanne?" Cora arched an eyebrow. "And on the subject of budget issues, I don't know if you've heard but Helena was in here yesterday and she told me that the library might be closing by year-end."

"Closing?" Jenna had successfully forgotten her problems now. The town library had been at the center of the community since their parents were children. "But...why? How?"

Cora shrugged. "This town relies on tourism more than anything else, and there hasn't been enough funding. The donors can only give so much, and the rest comes from the town. The mayor is thinking the property might be better served as another inn."

"Another inn!" Now Jenna couldn't believe what she was hearing. "But there are already so many." They lined Main Street, all similar in style with white cedar board siding and black painted shutters, the most popular being, of course, the Carriage House Inn, owned by Conway family's dear friends, the Bradfords.

"There's plenty of demand, and it would only help bring in more tourists and more money to the town." Cora sipped her cocoa. "Or so that's what Helena was told."

Helena had been a strict but loyal librarian for years, guarding the building with the same care as those who held the position before her. The historic property was always clean, warmly lit, and meticulously cared for, as were the books. Helena never shied from slapping a late fee on someone's account, but neither did she resist helping someone with research.

"There's a special town meeting this weekend." Cora glanced at the elf-shaped clock and stood. "You should come. I think my sisters and I would agree that it's important to do what we can to stop this from happening. Helena has always been a friend to us."

"I'll be there," Jenna agreed, slurping back the rest of her cocoa. Helena went back to their school days; like so many others in town, she wasn't just a passing face, but a part of their history. And the library was a part of the town's history.

Jenna stood and left the remaining cookies with Cora, knowing that she'd probably share them with Georgie next

time she saw her, and followed her cousin into the storefront, where all their troubles seemed to vanish as one beautifully decorated tree after another lit up the space.

"Who can't smile when they come in a place like this?" Jenna stopped to study a display case of Nutcracker-themed ornaments. The music from that ballet was a special favorite of hers.

"You're forgetting that I almost lost my store last year." Cora raised her eyebrows as she unlocked the front door and turned the sign. "That's what gives me some hope for Helena and the library."

Jenna felt better just hearing the conviction in Cora's tone. The Conway women were strong, independent business women who always came out on top. They could help their friend and this town.

But they couldn't help the pageant, she thought a little glumly.

"I think you're right, Cora," Jenna said, lifting her chin. "We'll figure something out. Christmas brings out the best in people, after all."

Or at least, some people…but probably not that new scrooge of a school principal.

Travis sat in his grandmother's house, watching the snow fall out the bay window while the fire crackled in the nearby fireplace. An old movie played in the distance—one of the holiday variety, and only because it made his grandmother happy.

He didn't see the hype, didn't understand all the energy that went into one day of the year that passed just as quickly as the others. But here, in Blue Harbor, it wasn't just a day. It was dragged out all month long if the decorations and the signs for the Winter Carnival and all its festivities were any indications.

At least here in the cozy house that he used to visit as a boy, the decorations were kept to a minimum, but that was only because he hadn't gotten into the attic yet to fetch the boxes, even though his grandmother had reminded him daily about it. He stood now, seeing no better time, but his Gran motioned for him to sit down again, and he knew better than to argue.

"You're going to miss the best part," Gran said from her favorite chair, a mere three feet from the television screen. Her knitting needles clicked as her fingers worked the yarn, but her eyes never strayed from the movie.

"You mean to tell me you've already seen this movie?"

She balked at him. "Only about fifty times! It's a classic. You haven't watched this one?"

Christmas movies weren't really his thing. "Why don't we find something you haven't watched before?" He'd love to see if a hockey game was playing.

Gran, however, shook her head. "This is one of the best holiday films ever made. The costumes. The scenery! I watch it every year. It's tradition."

Tradition. He was starting to hear that word a lot lately, something he couldn't connect with himself. His ex-girlfriend was fine with a wreath on the door, which they'd locked promptly behind them before boarding a plane to the Caribbean. And his mother...well, she didn't make time for silly things like decorating a tree or hanging garland. She was too busy trying to keep the lights on. And too proud to ask for help.

Travis warily studied the scarf his grandmother was making—something chunky and a little uneven in a shade of blue best suited for a newborn baby. He had the unsettling feeling that he might be the intended recipient.

His grandmother used to send a box every year—ranging from socks to hats, and he didn't have the heart to toss them any more than he had the nerve to wear them out in public. He could only imagine what the kids at school would have said about the variegated yarn, much less the oversized pom-poms. It was tough enough always being the new kid, seeing as they bounced around most years, sometimes even midyear. He was spared having to wear any of his grandmother's creations since she never visited around the holidays, choosing instead to stay in this small town where she had friends as close as family.

Maybe, even closer.

Now, watching as his grandmother laughed at something one of the actors in the film said, he couldn't help but wish that they'd spent more time together over the years.

All the more reason to make this year count, he told himself.

"Don't wear your fingers out," he half-joked, but there was concern in his tone, too. His Gran was getting up there in years, and she was his only living relative now. In many ways, she was all he had.

Gran, being Gran, harumphed, and stopped knitting only long enough to swat his comment away.

"No risk of that. I hope to finish some mittens in time for the tree lighting ceremony tomorrow night." The knitting needles clicked as her fingers moved a little less swiftly than they once had.

Travis hesitated. Everyone at the school had mentioned it in passing, as if it were something that couldn't be missed, even though he failed to see how it could be so exciting to stand around in the snow, waiting for some lights to come on a spruce tree. "Are you sure you're up to it? It's going to be cold—"

She looked up at him sharply. "I should think so! It's winter in northern Michigan!" She pursed her mouth and went back to her knitting. "But if you'd rather stay inside next to the nice warm fire, then you can drop me off at the town square and pick me up after the festivities."

She was calling his bluff and she knew it. They were both all too aware that she would never be able to get her wheelchair through the snow-covered park on her own, and he wouldn't let her, either.

"Speaking of fire, let me throw another log on it for you."

But his grandmother brushed him away before turning to him once the commercial break started. "It's fine. I'll be turning in soon. I had a long phone call with my friend Betty today that left me tired."

"Oh?" He knew that his grandmother usually looked so forward to the visits she had from people in town. The ringing of the telephone usually brought a smile to her face and boosted her energy for a bit, giving him a glimpse of the woman she used to be, the way that he remembered her when she was still young and she would regal him with stories of this town and even her youth. His visits to Blue Harbor were infrequent at best, usually during summer break when he was too young to stay home alone and his mother needed childcare, but those were memorable days. Good days, really.

"They're considering closing the library. The donor contributions haven't been enough in recent years and the town doesn't want to cover the rest when they could re-purpose the building."

"That's too bad." Travis frowned. Libraries had been a haven to him as a child, a consistency from school to school, despite everything else feeling different. It was there that he could find the same books, the same authors, bury himself in the same stories and escape the anxiety that came with always feeling like an outsider.

Now, as an educator, he placed great importance on libraries, and he encouraged the teachers and staff at the schools he'd worked in to do the same, supporting projects that included research that might not be found with a click of a home laptop or even smartphone.

"You remember, Travis, I used to bring you there every Saturday morning when you came to visit." His grandmother smiled at the memory. "You loved that train set in the children's section. I used to have to make sure you didn't pocket the caboose!"

Travis laughed along with his grandmother at the memory, but he was dismayed nonetheless. "Is the town really in trouble?"

"Tourism keeps booming. And that's just the problem." His grandmother raised an eyebrow. "It's sometimes easy to forget about the reason people want to visit our lovely town."

"And what is that?"

"Blue Harbor appeals to city people because of its history. Because we've preserved the buildings, taken care of them over time, given people something that they can count on when they return each year. This town hasn't changed much since I was a girl. Or since you were a boy."

Travis nodded pensively. His grandmother made a good point, but then, that never surprised him.

"This town is home to me, and that includes all the people and houses and businesses that are part of it," she said.

"Change should come with careful consideration, because once it happens...well, there's no going back."

Travis thought about all the changes that had occurred in his life—too many to count. Eventually, he forgot the places he'd lived, or they merged and he couldn't remember which apartment had the small balcony and which one had the loud neighbors, and he learned to focus on the present, not the past, and certainly not the future.

"There's no place like home, as the saying goes." Gran stifled a yawn as she resumed her knitting.

Travis watched the final minutes of the movie, but he wasn't paying attention to the dialogue. He was thinking about what his grandmother had said, about what made this town home to her, and he realized that he was almost thirty-five years old and that somehow, he still hadn't found that yet.

*

The Christmas choir was comprised of a group of local adults who gathered together each holiday season to spread cheer throughout the town of Blue Harbor. No Christmas Eve was complete without a round of door-to-door caroling, though a few homes had been crossed off the list in recent years, because contrary to Jenna's belief, not everyone enjoyed holiday music.

Like Mr. Dunne, Jenna thought, as she propped her music sheets on the stand and waited for the rest of the choir group to hang their coats.

"Have you seen this?" Candy—Jenna's newest family member, now that she was married to Uncle Dennis—

wasted no time in making her presence known. She held a piece of paper up to Jenna, which was surprisingly not another suggestion for a song they should sing at the tree lighting.

Jenna skimmed the flyer that was referring to the emergency town meeting this weekend and nodded. "I did. Such a shame. Helena must be heartbroken."

"*I'm* heartbroken!" Candy placed a hand dramatically to her chest, drawing attention to her festive sweater, which was red velvet, low-cut, as usual, and had a white-fir trim that gave a distinct impression of Mrs. Clause. A less than traditional Mrs. Clause, but all the same, Mrs. Clause.

"You know that I am an avid supporter of that library! Why, I must take out…ten, fifteen books a month!"

And forget to return them, Jenna refrained from saying. Instead, Candy's stepdaughters had been covering her tab and simultaneously shoving library books into their handbags every time they visited their father, which they later returned to a relieved Helena.

"Bella's Books is a wonderful store, don't get me wrong," Candy continued, and Jenna wasn't about to argue with her. Her cousin Isabella had one of the quaintest shops in town, and she pulled in the community with her story hours and poetry readings, and monthly book clubs, too. Candy participated in the latter two, of course, though her poetry was known to raise some eyebrows. "But the library obviously has a much bigger selection of my genre."

Jenna handed her aunt back the sheet of paper. "I know how much you enjoy your romance novels, Candy," she said with a smile. "Are you going to the town meeting?"

"As if anyone needs to ask! I understand the need for tourism, of course, but if we don't preserve what makes this town special, eventually, all those weekenders and summer people will stop coming."

Jenna nodded. Candy could sometimes be surprisingly wise. "All the more reason to make the tree lighting event extra special then." She glanced at the group that had already assembled according to height and waited for Candy to take the hint.

But Candy wasn't finished yet. Since joining the group a few weeks ago, Candy often had something to contribute, in addition to a high falsetto and a need to be heard above all the other carolers.

"I was thinking that maybe this year, we could all agree to wear something different than our wool coats and scarves," Candy said, biting her lower lip.

Jenna frowned. "Like uniforms? I'm not so sure that people would go for that."

"I mean costumes."

Jenna pulled in a breath. Candy was never one to back down when her mind was set on something, and there was no telling what costumes she had in mind. Santa's elves? Jenna was a fan of costumes for children but she wasn't so sure the look would translate for the adults—or that the rest of the group would agree.

"Let's talk about it after the rehearsal," Jenna said with a smile. "We need all the practice we can get before tomorrow night!"

"I'm just so grateful that Amelia gave me the time off work to participate in this!" Candy trilled as she took her spot—front and center—with the rest of the group.

Yes, and Jenna's cousin Amelia was all too grateful that Jenna had welcomed Candy into the choir this year so that she could have a little peace and quiet in her kitchen at the Firefly Café, at least for a couple of hours a week, where Candy tended to sing while she cooked her famous cheese biscuits. Amelia had even offered Jenna dinner on the house for the entire month of December in appreciation, Jenna remembered as she turned to the first carol in her binder. An old favorite, even if she did have to remind Candy to not drag out the last note quite so long each time.

The Firefly Café was one of her favorite spots in town, and Amelia was one of her favorite people. When Jenna's sister Brooke had moved back to town last spring, she'd made a promise to her sisters to get out more, but after-school piano lessons often ran late, and she'd assumed her holiday season would be packed between choir rehearsals and the school pageant. Maybe she'd have to follow in Cora's footsteps, make some new traditions. Next year she'd probably be so busy with the pageant that she wouldn't even have time to drop by the café. Maybe next year, when Suzanne was back, she'd be running the whole show!

She walked to the piano and took her seat on the bench, hovering her foot over the pedals. She closed her eyes as her fingers found the keys without having to look at the notes, and began to play as her group of neighbors, friends, and family lifted their voices.

At times like this, she was reminded that Christmas in Blue Harbor was perfect. And worth staying for, too.

*

Jenna's optimism only lasted until the last choir member (Candy, of course) had left the building. Her parents' house was close to the center of town, and rather than return to her empty apartment, she walked down Main Street to Spruce, taking in all the lights and sparkling trees in people's front windows.

Her parents had wasted no time in setting up their tree—not that they ever had. The weekend after Thanksgiving was their tradition growing up, though in recent years Jenna often had too many piano lessons to help out for long. Gabby was usually tied down at the flower shop—wreaths and centerpieces were in high demand this time of year—and Brooke had only moved back from New York last spring.

Jenna paused outside the small picket fence that divided their property from the sidewalk and admired her parents' work, wishing that she had made the time to help out, that she hadn't put so much effort into planning a pageant that wasn't even going to take place.

Technically, she didn't live here, but this was home, and she knew her parents would be offended if she knocked before entering. Instead, she turned the front knob, not surprised to find it unlocked because her parents had lived in this small town all their lives and trusted that everything would just continue as it always had, even though change was clearly in the air, at least for her.

"Hello!" she called out as she wiped the snow off her boots.

"Jenna?" Her mother quickly appeared in the hall. "Well, this is a surprise. We just ate. Can I offer you something?"

Jenna shook her head, then, on second thought, nodded. A home-cooked meal sure beat whatever she might make for herself back in her tiny kitchen. "That would be really nice after the day I've had."

"Uh-oh," her mother said. "Well, you hang up your coat and I'll heat up a plate."

Jenna set her wet things on the radiator to dry, as she had as a kid, and then met her mother in the kitchen. The island and oak table were anchored by poinsettias and pine cones. "Gabby's work?"

"Of course!" Her mother smiled as she set a plate on the counter. "Now that your sister has finally hired an assistant, she doesn't require my services as much, but I can't stop showing up at the shop anyway, so I figured I may as well buy a few things."

Jenna fell into a stool and picked up her fork. Roasted chicken with mashed potatoes. She couldn't complain.

"So," her mother said, leaning over the other side of the island. "How's the pageant coming along?"

Jenna swallowed a bite of food and realized that she couldn't eat it, regardless of how good it tasted. "There isn't going to be a pageant this year."

Her mother pulled back in surprise. "What? But why not?"

"Apparently people have complained that it's…stale."

Her mother narrowed her eyes. "There's nothing stale about a tradition. That's the whole point, isn't it? For people to have the same thing to look forward to, year after year?"

"Try telling that to Principal Dunne." Jenn sighed. "Suzanne left. Family emergency. Now there's a temporary principal and he, well, he isn't a fan of what I do."

"Oh, honey." Her mother took her hand and squeezed it. "He just doesn't know talent when he sees it."

Jenna didn't point out that those were the same words her mother had said all those years ago when she'd bombed in her audition for the music college.

"The worst part of it all is that it's Mr. Pritchard's last year. I was hoping to do something special for him."

"Well, just because this new principal doesn't want to have a school pageant, that doesn't mean he can stop you from honoring Mr. Pritchard."

"And how would I do that?"

"Have your own pageant!"

Jenna considered this for a moment, then shook her head. "I don't see how I could do that. I don't have the resources." The costumes all belonged to the school. More like they were rented by the school.

"You could figure it out. You have the Christmas choir. What's to stop you from having a children's choir?"

Jenna could think of a few things. Her pride. Her wounded ego. Her lack of funding. Her creeping self-doubt that maybe this guy was right, maybe she wasn't any good, that maybe she'd been fooling herself to think that people liked what she did with the pageant.

"It's a little late in the season," she said, trying to think of how much time she had.

"So? This is a small town, and it wouldn't take long for word to spread."

"We'd need a venue," Jenna said, considering her options now that the school auditorium was most definitely not one.

"What about the Winter Carnival? Everyone attends anyway. It would be the perfect opportunity for the children to perform."

"You don't think that the kids will be too full of sugar or too tired from all the activities?" Jenna frowned, thinking of the year she'd had one too many hot chocolates followed by a bumpy ride in the sledding races.

"It's the most festive event of the year," her mother said. "Think about it, at least. You do amazing work with those kids at the summer music camp, and they love having you at the school, too."

"Loved," Jenna corrected. "I'm worried those days are behind me now." She hesitated before adding, "Like other things in my life."

"Life is full of setbacks and you've had your share," her mother said firmly but kindly. "You've always found a way to come out the other side and you will again. You love music, Jenna, and that's what has never changed."

No, it hadn't. Even when she'd lost her nerve and her confidence, she had never lost her passion.

"You always kept believing in yourself. And Christmas is, above all things, a time for believing."

Jenna smiled her first smile in days and picked up her fork again. Leave it to her mother to state the obvious.

Jenna's sisters were already waiting for her near the entrance to the town square when she arrived at the tree lighting ceremony, harried and slightly out of breath. Her lesson with Anthony DeMarco had run longer than usual on account of the poor child's frustration with the final notes of "Jingle Bells." Jenna didn't have the heart to tell him that they could finish up next week, but that had left her little time to get ready for tonight.

Still, her hair was brushed, she was wearing the warm, cashmere sweater in a perfect shade of cranberry under her matching wool coat, and her leather tote was full of music for tonight's event, even though she had all the songs memorized by now. Ever since a fifth-grade recital when she blanked on the second verse of a piece she'd practiced ten times a day for weeks, she always made sure to have her sheets with her, just in case.

"Were you waiting long?" Jenna noticed that the crowd was already pretty full for the hour. They had purposefully agreed to meet at this time so they'd have a chance to chat before Jenna took her seat at the piano that had been placed inside the big gazebo. She was happy that the paths had been cut and salted. Tonight's ankle boots were fashionable for piano pedals but not slippery snow.

"Only long enough to see the line for mulled wine quadruple," Gabby said with a wry grin.

"I'm sure that Britt will make an exception if we smile nicely," Brooke only half-joked. Now that their cousin Britt and her fiancé Robbie Bradford were running the Conway family orchard and winery, they'd taken the business to a new level, and Jenna and her sisters were happy to support it as was the rest of the town.

"Let's get in line now before it grows any longer," Jenna suggested as they followed the smell of warm, sweet spice. She wouldn't have any wine tonight, not when she had a concert to perform, but she certainly wouldn't say no to a hot mug of cider, another Conway specialty.

"Look, there's Maddie!" Gabby shot up a mitten-covered hand and started gesturing frantically to their cousin. "Hurry up before someone gets behind us!"

Maddie did as she was told and jogged and slid through the snow-covered park, managing to join them in line before two other couples followed suit.

"You don't have to work tonight?" Jenna asked, gesturing to some of the other kiosks that were selling drinks and food.

Maddie shook her head. "I don't want to compete with Amelia, and I could use a night off anyway. Besides, Cole's meeting me here soon once he finishes up a project in Pine Falls."

She smiled at the mention of her boyfriend, whom she'd now been dating for over a year. Jenna pondered on that as the line progressed a few feet. So much had transpired in Maddie's life in a relatively short time, between starting a business and dating Cole, and the same could be said for Brooke and Gabby as well. Whereas Jenna...well, Jenna had been content doing the same thing each day. Waking up, practicing her music, and teaching the town's youth. The most exciting thing that had happened to her all year was moving into her new apartment over Brooke's wedding dress shop.

She never complained about it, and it rarely bothered her, but that was until one of the things that filled her otherwise quiet existence had been taken away.

She glanced at the piano tucked beside the big tree, donated by Bob's tree lot, and thought again about her mother's idea to host a children's choir. If she wanted to do it, she'd have to act fast. Christmas was just around the corner now, and tonight they'd be kicking off the season.

Maddie elbowed her as they moved up in line. "Hey, how did the meeting go with Suzanne? Did my cookies help sweeten the deal?"

Jenna felt her spirits sink. She hadn't wanted to discuss this tonight, not when she was about to perform, and not when this was a day that she looked forward to all year. But now her sisters were looking at her with curious expressions, and there were still at least six groups in front of them in line, and well, they'd end up hearing the news soon enough, likely by the time they reached the kiosk. Keira Bradford was not only one of Jenna's favorite pupils but also a student at the school who had been looking very forward to this year's pageant. No doubt that Robbie would be offering a kind word or two with a mug of hot cider, possibly on the house, because he was like that.

And because he was almost family.

"Suzanne has been replaced with a temporary principal," Jenna said with a pinch of her lips. "I'm afraid that even your delicious cookies couldn't soften the heart of that Scrooge."

In front of them, a man cleared his throat. Now both of her sisters had given her their full attention, and Maddie had completely stopped glancing toward Main Street in hopes of seeing Cole.

"They've…they've canceled the pageant this year." Just saying the words reminded her of the awful truth.

"No!" Maddie said.

"Oh, yes," Jenna said bitterly. "It would seem that not everyone values traditions."

"Even Christmas traditions?" Brooke shook her head.

"My services are being replaced with a digital recording." Jenna could barely get out the words. "The kids will sing a song to their parents during their holiday parties."

"But…but the children love that pageant!" Maddie said.

"Apparently I'm stale," Jenna said. "Like yesterday's bread."

Now Gabby set a hand on her arm. "Oh, honey. Other than seeing their kids sing and jingle a bell in a cute little costume, you're the reason most people looked forward to the pageant! I'm sure this old curmudgeon is half-deaf. He'd have to be to turn down your participation."

The man in front of them coughed. Jenna took a step back. The last thing she needed was to catch a cold and further ruin her holidays.

"He's not old. He's…well, he was actually sort of cute." Jenna almost resented having to admit this. Cute and cold.

Now Maddie's eyes gleamed in a way only they could, given the circumstances.

Jenna swatted her. "Maddie! He fired me. He didn't even give me a chance. Looks aside, the man clearly has a heart of ice."

"Absolutely!" Gabby said with a firm nod. "At least his job is temporary."

Jenna found little solace in this statement, but there was some nonetheless. "Yes, with any luck, he'll be out of town just as quickly as he came into it. From what I've gathered he won't be making *any* friends along the way."

Her family all nodded along. Absolutely, yes, absolutely.

From across the park, Keira came running through the snow toward the kiosk, her cheeks nearly as bright a pink as her puffer coat.

"Principal Dunne! Principal Dunne!"

The man in front of them turned and flashed a wide smile to Keira. "Hello, there, Keira! So nice to see you!"

Principal Dunne? Jenna's breath stalled when she glanced at her sisters and cousin, whose wide-eyed expressions matched her alarm.

"My teacher said we could vote on our class song for the holiday party. I nominated a song and it won!"

"Wonderful." The man had the nerve to actually smile. It was a wolfish, Scrooge-like smile if ever Jenna saw one. A smirk, really.

She waited to see if he'd turn around to prove his point, but he stayed put. Maybe he hadn't heard them. Maybe she could just slowly back away, out of line, and sprint to the piano where she really should get set up, even if the tree wouldn't be lit for another half hour.

Jenna and her sisters edged up in line. Her cheeks burned so much that she considered unbuttoning her coat. She watched as Principal Dunne turned his head, his face now in profile to them, looking around at the crowd that continued to gather.

She waited, hoping he would turn around, edge up in line, but no. No, that was not how her week was going.

With a lift of his eyebrow, his mouth quirked and he turned to face her head-on, the merriment in his dark eyes snuffing out her last hope that he hadn't caught any part of her conversation.

"Jenna. Nice to see you again."

She pinched her mouth. She could hardly say the same, but that would be impolite, and besides, Maddie was now nudging her side with her elbow.

"Principal Dunne." She nodded. "These are my sisters, Gabby and Brooke. And my cousin, Maddie."

"Travis." He grinned. A genuine, even friendly grin, or so she might have said if she didn't know his true spirit.

There were handshakes all around, and Maddie did a terrible job of hiding her smile as they edged up in line. Thankfully, it was Travis's turn now, and he ordered two hot ciders, which gave Jenna a moment of pause.

She didn't know what was more surprising: that he would attend a Christmas event, or that he wasn't here alone!

"Have a wonderful time, ladies. Jenna, nice seeing you again." He grinned again, until his eyes crinkled with what Jenna might only call mischief, and she cursed under her breath the moment he was gone, cutting across the snow, carrying two steaming paper cups to his date.

"Pity the woman he's here with tonight," Jenna remarked as they approached the stand.

"With a face like that, there's nothing to pity!" Maddie edged up closer to Jenna. "You weren't exaggerating when you said he was cute."

"Cute, and a curmudgeon. Just like you said." Jenna inched to the side while the orders were placed, but she couldn't resist darting her eyes over the crowd, in the direction that Travis had walked. Idle curiosity, she told herself. It would certainly be interesting to see what woman in town would put up with such a cold-blooded man, however attractive.

"You all met the new principal just now?" It was Robbie who asked the question. "Keira said he's great with the kids, but she's pretty bummed about not having a pageant this year. It was her year to be an angel!"

Jenna gave Robbie a long look. There was a lot she could say on this topic, but the line was long and she really did need to take her post soon. She always liked to have a few minutes to prepare before a performance, to get the feel of the keys, to assess her positioning, and take some calming breaths. Some events were comfortable, especially here in Blue Harbor, where everyone was her friend.

But having Travis Dunne in the crowd tonight, she couldn't help but feel judged again. And even a little rejected.

"If I told Keira there might still be a chance for her to perform in front of a big crowd this Christmas, do you think she'd be interested?" she blurted. Her heart was beating faster. Could she really do this? Put on a show, all on her own?

Robbie nodded, looking a little confused. "I'm sure. Why? What did you have in mind?"

"Oh…just gathering information," Jenna said as she stepped aside for the next couple. She looked across the town square, taking in the lights and the excitement, reminding herself that this event wouldn't happen again until next year.

Travis Dunne might have made it his personal mission to steal some of her Christmas spirit, but she'd be darned if she let him take away that pageant from the kids, or overshadow tonight for her, either.

*

So he was a Scrooge, was he? Travis didn't know whether to be insulted or flattered. He did know that he was very happy his grandmother had been warming herself near one of the bonfires that had been set up throughout the town square, and that she, therefore, didn't happen to hear that conversation, because as much as he might not match her enthusiasm for the holidays, he certainly intended to give her a wonderful Christmas.

He carried the two cups of steaming cider to the small circle of benches that had been set up near the blazing fire, close enough to view the tree lighting with a relatively unobstructed view. His grandmother was staring into the flames, a faraway look in her eyes when he sat down. She barely noticed him until he extended a hand containing a paper cup.

"Careful. It's hot."

"Oh, I'll be fine," she tutted, brushing away his concerns.

And she would be, he knew, but still, he worried. It was her brazen attitude that had landed her in the wheelchair in the first place. She'd always been stubborn and independent. Losing her husband just a year after Travis's mother was born had made her resilient, she said. She'd never remarried and prided herself on her accomplishments. She was a pioneer of her generation, she claimed. She was also unwilling to admit that she ever needed help.

Much like her daughter, Travis thought with a heavy heart. He'd watched her struggle firsthand over the years, a single mother who was doing the best she could without a lot of resources. He offered to help, but she would just give him that worried look and tell him that she was fine, even when it was clear that she was tired and anxious. He didn't ask for anything, instead. He downplayed the newest video game systems, told his mother he didn't like the new fashion trends, and never put much focus on birthdays. Or Christmas.

Eventually, he even convinced himself.

"Sure took you long enough," his grandmother said as she sipped her cider. "It's a wonder it's not cold by now."

Travis grinned. This was his grandmother's way of showing she was tough, not weak, and he found amusement in it, rather than annoyance. "I ran into someone I know."

Now his grandmother looked at him with interest. "A woman?"

He hesitated, not liking the sudden hope that filled her expression. "Yes, it was a woman. Someone from a school meeting."

She nodded her approval. "This town is full of pretty women."

"So are most towns," he said with an easy smile. And that didn't mean he was going to start dating again, even though he knew that his grandmother was pushing for something more than that. No, she wanted marriage. A front-row seat so she could die in peace, or so she liked to remind him every few days.

"Yes, but this town also has me," Gran said with a mischievous smile. "And you'll be hard-pressed to find a town with better Christmas traditions."

Travis sipped his drink. He didn't have the heart to admit to his grandmother that he didn't match her enthusiasm when it came to the holiday any more than he was willing to admit his part in deciding to cancel the school's pageant—even if that was hardly his fault. He was just the messenger, doing the fiscally conservative thing. Making the most of a difficult situation. When he looked at it that way, he'd found a way to still salvage some form of the concert for the children.

But something in the way Jenna had stared at him tonight made him think that she, at least, didn't see it that way.

They were interrupted by a few newcomers to their bonfire—two women he knew from the school, though their names escaped him. From beside him, his grandmother made a strong showing of clearing her throat, and he refused to so much as glance her way, knowing that her facial expression would equally lack subtlety.

Instead, he smiled at the two women, who reminded him that they were Lauren and Carly by way of introduction to his grandmother.

"It's so nice having a fresh face at work," the school nurse, Carly, said, and her coworker elbowed her at that. "Do you think you'll stay in Blue Harbor?"

Now, Travis could feel the heat of his grandmother's gaze, burning hotter than the logs in the fire. He took a sip of his drink to stall and shrugged. "Not sure, really."

No was the real answer. He didn't stay anywhere, at least not for long. After moving around so much as a kid, he'd gotten used to the change of scenery, felt the itch for a fresh start every couple of years, grew restless if he was kept in one place for too long.

It was always easier not to get too comfortable, he'd learned at a young age. Better not to make friends you'd have to leave. Better not to join a team that you would later let down. Better not to look back.

He was almost grateful when the crowd quieted down and the topic of his love life could be put on hold—until he saw a group of choir singers, led by Jenna, gather near the tree. The mayor said a few words as Jenna took her seat at the piano bench, her dark hair held back in waves that cascaded down the back of her red coat that matched the scarves each member of the choir wore.

As the speech wrapped up, Jenna held her fingers over the keys. Even from this distance, he could see her take a moment to pull in a breath, but as the music started, any sign of nerves disappeared. She played with ease, and even joy, and the music was like nothing he'd heard before, at least not firsthand. The choir began to sing and all eyes in the crowd were on the tree, which would light up at any moment, but there was something about the quiet, the snow, and the way that the music filled the space, that made it impossible for Travis to look at anything or anyone but Jenna.

The song finished just as the tree came to life and the crowd whooped in delight and then broke out in cheer. Travis looked at his grandmother, seeing the joy shining in her eyes when she looked up at the tree, and just for that moment, he saw a glimpse of her younger, sturdier self, and maybe, even a shadow of his mother.

Travis joined the crowd in their applause, but it wasn't the tree that impressed him or held his attention.

Two things had slipped his observation at that rather awkward first meeting: Jenna Conway was a beautiful piano player. She was also, he couldn't help but note, a rather beautiful woman.

Jenna knew most of the children in Blue Harbor from her work at the school, but she took a special liking to her private lesson students, in particular her cousin Britt's soon-to-be stepdaughter, Keira, who had only been taking lessons for a few months but whose enthusiasm was rarely matched.

"I want to be able to play 'Carol of the Bells' by Christmas Eve," Keira told her when they finished working on her scales.

Jenna hesitated. She didn't want to discourage her pupil, but that was a particularly difficult piece, and she wasn't sure she would be able to find beginner-level sheet music for it. Still, she smiled at Keira and said, "Let me see what I can find for next week. You'll have to practice for a song like that."

Keira nodded earnestly. "I will. I'll practice every day."

"Okay then." Jenna smiled as she rose from the bench. The secondhand piano that had been with her for years sat near the window of her apartment that overlooked Main Street. It was already dusk and the lights from town twinkled through the glass. "I told your dad and Britt that I'd bring you over to the town hall with me after your lesson.

Be sure to button your coat. The temperature is supposed to drop tonight."

"Jenna?" Keira pulled her coat from the hook near the door and carefully buttoned each button. "Do you think if we hurry we can look in the window of the shop downstairs first?"

Jenna laughed. She'd taken over the apartment lease from her sister after Brooke reunited with her husband, and the location above Something Blue was a frequent distraction with some of her young students, especially those who enjoyed princess stories.

"Better than that. We can go inside. I promised Brooke I'd walk over to the meeting with her." She handed Keira her hat and they hurried down the internal stairs that led to the back of the storefront. The lights were still on in the boutique, even though the business was closed for the day, and Brooke was fluffing a tulle veil when they entered the store, which glistened and sparkled nearly as much as the lights reflecting off the snow outside.

"I can't wait to be a bride!" Keira cried, running from one display to another, knowing from her recent visits to the shop with Britt that she could look but not touch. Still, Brooke seemed to stiffen each time her little hands went out.

Jenna didn't blame her. The gowns were stunning, each one unique, and Brooke had created a winter wonderland feel to the space in recent weeks.

"You get to be a flower girl," Brooke reminded her as she started to flick off the lights. She slipped into her light-grey wool coat which was more fashionable than it was practical and brushed her blond hair free from the collar.

The wedding wouldn't be until the spring when the cherry trees were in bloom; of course, Britt and Robbie would be married at the orchard, where they'd reunited and now worked side by side, growing the business that had been in the Conway family for generations and now likely would be for many more.

"Just thinking of spring makes me sad that Christmas is almost over," Jenna said with a laugh.

"It's only the first week of December!" Brooke shook her head and ushered them out the front door.

"My favorite time of the year," Jenna said.

Keira picked up on the frown in her tone and shook her hand. "Are you sad about the pageant being canceled? I'm sad. But at least we get to sing to our parents at our class party, even if there won't be costumes or piano music."

Jenna didn't want to dampen the evening. It was Christmastime, and it was especially magical for children.

"How can I be sad with all these wonderful decorations and lights?" Jenna swept her arms wide, embracing the charming street that came to life this time of year.

Jenna and Keira admired the window display while Brooke locked up the shop—a winter dress under the fur stole was with a mesh long-sleeved overlay on a satin gown covered in what must be tens of thousands of tiny crystals. It looked like a snowflake. It was certainly as unique as one.

"I think if I ever get married, that is what I want my dress to look like," Jenna said wistfully. "And I'd have

Christmas carols for the ceremony. Candles against the snow."

"Sounds like you have it all planned out!" Brooke half-joked.

"Only because I live above this shop and I'm related to you!" It was true that Jenna had never given much thought to marriage or finding love before—she'd been too busy with her music, too caught up in the joy of her fingers moving along the keys. She assumed at some point she'd meet someone. It just hadn't happened yet. If it didn't, she had her music. She knew not everyone could claim something else for their first and truest love.

"I hope you do get married soon!" Keira said earnestly.

Jenna looked down at her as they joined hands and began to walk. "And why is that?"

"Because I want to have another chance to be a flower girl!"

Jenna and Brooke laughed. The town hall wasn't far, and a line of people was already filing through the front doors. By the time they made it to the community room downstairs, Jenna realized that all the chairs were filled.

"Is it usually like this?" She turned to Brooke, who looked just as surprised as she was. "I've never attended one of these meetings before."

"Seems like the library's fate is creating quite a stir," Brooke said. The question being, was everyone here in favor of keeping it?

Keira craned her neck through the crowd of people who were inching closer together. "I see my dad near the front of the room!"

"Go ahead," Jenna said, watching her run forward to the right side of the room where most of Jenna's cousins and their significant others were already gathered. Gabby had already joined them.

"I think Kyle saved me a seat." Brooke gave her husband a wave and then winced at Jenna, seeking approval.

"Go on. I'm fine!" And she was. She didn't mind being on her own. Besides, here in Blue Harbor, she knew everyone. Why, she could probably look around and name every single person in this room. Including…

Oh, brother. Travis Dunne. What was *he* doing here?

Jenna quickly shifted behind one of the taller men in the room, happy that most people were still bundled in their winter coats, lending an easy shield. Still, her eyes flicked to the right as the mayor started to speak, wondering if Travis had seen her.

She breathed easier when she saw that his attention was fixed firmly on the front of the room, where, following a call for understanding from the townspeople, the mayor asked for comments.

Not surprisingly, Candy's hand was the first to shoot up in the crowd.

"I think that this year's Winter Carnival proceeds should go toward the library."

A murmur went up in the crowd, and Jenna couldn't be sure if it was one of agreement or not. Still, Candy posed an interesting idea, not that Jenna was surprised. Candy was the type of person who didn't back down when she set her mind to something, and as someone who hadn't grown up in this town, she was partial enough to see it in a different way than most people in the room could.

Other than Travis Dunne.

Jenna narrowed her eyes at the man who was so quick to dismiss a beloved Christmas tradition and then shifted her gaze back to Candy, who was now moving to the podium, the Christmas lights on her multi-colored, battery-operated necklace guiding her way.

Jenna caught the glance shared by Britt and Amelia and couldn't help but smile. It was people like Candy who made this town special.

Candy took a moment to collect herself by fluffing her curls and clearing her throat. "The Winter Carnival attracts locals and tourists alike. It's because of the festivities like the carnival that people want to live here *and* want to visit. But it's also because of places like the library. If this town was all about tourism, it would lose its sense of authenticity, its charm. Maybe even its heart. So what do you say? And it doesn't have to stop with the carnival! We could turn all the other events we cherish this month into a fundraising effort, maybe even think of some new ones, too."

Amelia was the first to stand. "Firefly Café will donate all of its proceeds from the carnival toward saving the library."

Candy beamed and yanked a marker from the mayor's hand. In the front row, Helena looked like she was near tears from relief as Candy wrote on the whiteboard in her loopy handwriting, dotting each "I" with a heart, as was her way.

Maddie stood next. "Buttercream Bakery will do the same."

Cora and Britt were next, exhausting Candy's immediate family until Bella rose. "As a bookstore owner, it is my civic duty to support the literary arts. I don't have a stand at the Winter Carnival, but I'd like to volunteer my time, anything I can do or create to make sure that this is the biggest, most profitable, and most wonderful Winter Carnival that this town has ever seen."

The room broke out in cheer, and soon Candy was scribbling down names of vendors who would volunteer their services faster than she could write. Soon, there were new ideas for making the carnival bigger and better than all the years before, and fundraising ideas that would allow residents to participate in the holiday and help out at the same time—crafts that were typically sold at the carnival were now being donated. The wreath-making event that Gabby hosted each year would now be for the cause.

"We can do a special shopping day!" Candy suggested. "All participating shops can offer a discount. It will draw in people from neighboring towns."

"And a gift-wrapping event," Robbie's mother called out, waving her hand in the air. "We'll host in the lobby of the Carriage House. There's plenty of room for extra tables and chairs to be brought in for the day."

"And I'll donate the paper!" Cora chimed in.

"It can all be part of a bigger, longer Winter Carnival, with the carnival itself capping things off before the holiday!" Candy clapped at her own idea and several others joined in.

The effort from everyone was enormous, and from the look on Helena's face, unexpected. But then, this was Blue Harbor. How could Jenna have ever doubted that everyone would pull together in a time of need?

Maybe it was her conversation with Keira tonight, or maybe it was the energy in the room, or maybe it was Travis Dunne's presence, reminding her of what she was fighting for that prompted Jenna's hand to shoot up. Candy called on her before Jenna had a chance to change her mind.

"Some of you may know that the school pageant was canceled this year, but that doesn't mean we have to deny the children a chance to perform. I'm happy to organize a children's choir for anyone interested. No charge, just another event to draw people to the carnival."

From across the aisle, Jenna's mother beamed at her, but it was Candy who proclaimed, "It will be a main attraction of the carnival! I'll give it a special place on the new signs."

It seemed to be agreed upon before Jenna could even say anything more, and from every side of her, people nodded their approval, some evening thanking her for the idea.

The mayor stood, looking pleased and proud. "My assistant is putting out volunteer sheets at the back of the room. Please sign up for whatever you can contribute—whether it be services, food, or just your time. If there's any hope for funding the library, this is it!"

Jenna clapped, feeling all warm and fuzzy again at the way this town pulled together when it was needed the most, and, because she was already at the back of the room, hurried to the table near the stairs in the hallway to sign the volunteer sheets, where she grabbed a blank sheet and wrote "Children's Choir" at the very top. She was very familiar with the carnival's offerings, as well as the many events that the town hosted, and she was already looking forward to some of the new ideas that had been tossed around. And seeing as she had extra time on her hands now that her services were no longer needed at the school, she signed up for as many things as she could, feeling better already.

A purpose was always a good thing when it came to distracting from life's disappointments. And helping a friend was always something she'd make time for, especially at Christmas.

She glanced back at the crowd slowly pushing through the doors as she set a hand on the banister, noticing Mr. Dunne at the back of the crowd. That man may have no Christmas spirit, but she'd be darned if she let him ruin her holidays.

*

Travis watched as Jenna hurried up the stairs, her red scarf trailing behind her. He had wondered if she'd be at the town meeting tonight—and assumed that she would. She'd made it clear that this town was important to her, and it would seem that she wasn't alone in thinking that.

Looking around at the turnout as he filed out of the room, he was surprised at how many people had come out tonight—many of the faces he recognized from last night's tree lighting. Several had already stopped him to ask if his grandmother was in attendance, and he'd replied with what was becoming the semi-truth, that he was here on her behalf.

Blue Harbor had never been his home—he couldn't say which town or city ever was—but it was important to his grandmother and that made it important to him.

With that, he stopped at the volunteer table, knowing that his grandmother would have words to say if he didn't sign her up for at least two events. He scanned the sheets, knowing that the craft fair would be an excellent opportunity for her to unload some of her knitted goods (preferably that baby blue scarf with what was quickly appearing to be a ruffled edge), and knew that she would probably find enjoyment in the wreath-making event too.

He frowned when his hand slid over the children's choir sign-up list, which was already two rows deep, and then, before he could think about it further, moved onto the next form.

Winter Carnival planning committee. That seemed easy enough, and management came naturally to him. But that wasn't the real motivation as he picked up the pen. No, it was the name signed in loopy cursive, feminine, neat, and very legible: Jenna Conway.

Before he could give it another thought, he signed his name below hers.

*

Jenna spotted Mr. Pritchard standing at the doors, adjusting the buttons on his coat before he braved the cold. She hurried her pace, not just from anyone who might be behind her on the stairs, but because she'd been eager to speak to her former music teacher ever since the disastrous meeting earlier in the week.

"Mr. Pritchard!"

He turned and smiled at her and she couldn't help but do the same, even though the mere thought of the pageant put her in a funk these days.

"I've been hoping to talk to you," she said as she approached. "About the pageant. You must be so disappointed. I hope I wasn't overstepping back there."

"Not in the slightest!" He fumbled with the last of his buttons with trembling hands, and with a wash of sadness, she wondered if he was still able to play the piano. She knew that he'd stopped teaching private lessons years ago, which had allowed her to fill that void here in town. But now, seeing how he'd aged so much since last year's holiday event, she couldn't help but long for the days when she was still his pupil, he was still able to pursue the music he loved, and that her future still felt bright, thanks to his encouragement.

"I think the children are okay with the change for this year." He looked at her with kind blue eyes. "But I'm sorry that you're disappointed, dear. You always put such special care into the pageant, and this choir is a wonderful compromise. I hope you know how much I appreciated it and enjoyed working with you. I'm sad that those times have to come to an end, but grateful that we had the experience. It's not every day that a teacher gets to work side by side with his former pupil."

Jenna frowned at his word choice. "I know you're retiring this year, but that doesn't have to be the end of your contribution to the pageant. I'm sure the school would welcome the opportunity to have you help out again next year."

He tilted his head. "Ah, so you didn't hear?"

Jenna's heart skipped a beat. "Hear what?"

Mr. Pritchard sighed. "The music department is at risk of being cut, my dear. The board will be voting on it in their final meeting of the calendar year later this month. There just isn't enough room in the budget for everything, and the resources have to be allocated elsewhere. I suppose I should be relieved that the timing lines up with my retirement, but it saddens me that so much has changed since I first started working there."

Jenna blinked back tears. No music department for the children? How could the board allow such a thing? It had been music that had taken her out of her shell, when she was a shy girl with shaky confidence, always feeling like she was living in the shadow of her bright and shiny sisters. They hadn't intended for her to feel that way, but it had happened all the same. She was quieter, she liked to be home, and she hadn't found her niche, not like them.

But then, thanks to the man standing before her, she'd discovered music. A chance to express herself, and even untapped talent, as he liked to say.

Jenna glanced over her shoulder to where the crowd was starting to come up the stairs and then back to Mr. Pritchard. "Did Suzanne tell you this or Travis Dunne?"

"Principal Dunne," Mr. Pritchard said. "Though I'm not sure Suzanne will be returning, or if she was just waiting to deliver the news after my retirement. We go way back, of course."

Of course. And that would be a reason for Suzanne to hold back such devastating news rather than taint Mr. Pritchard's final year at the school.

"Have you spoken to the board members?"

"I'm afraid with my planned retirement, my opinion wouldn't hold much weight," he explained.

"Then I can speak to them!" She searched his face. "If you think it will help?"

"Oh, Jenna, that's kind of you, but I'm afraid it would take more than one person, and more than a few dollars, from what I understand, too."

"But it's not certain yet," she said, hearing the desperation creep into her tone. "There's still a chance they will decide to cut back on other things."

Mr. Pritchard's gaze was steady and long. Finally, with a kind smile, he said, "One can hope. Especially at Christmas."

"Can I walk you to the car?" Jenna asked. She needed fresh air to clear her head, and with the slippery sidewalks, she wouldn't mind making sure that her favorite teacher made it safely.

"I can't think of better company," Mr. Pritchard said with a smile. "Christmas can be lonely for an old widower."

Jenna slipped her arm through his. She knew this was his first holiday without his wife. All the more reason she would be sure to make the children's choir an event to remember. She'd have them sing all of his favorite songs. He deserved that much, but so much more.

"Then you must volunteer for some of the fundraising efforts, especially the choir. I would welcome your help, and I've learned over the years that keeping busy is the best way to get your mind off your troubles."

"Such a wise girl," Mr. Pritchard said.

She gave his hand a little pat as they stepped out into the winter air. "I learned from the best."

And that was precisely why she wasn't going to let Mr. Pritchard's music department be sacrificed if she could help it.

The gingerbread event was a local favorite amongst Blue Harbor locals. Each December, the members of the community joined in the basement of the town hall for a day of baking and decorating. Unlike past seasons, this year, each gingerbread house that was made would be put up for auction at the end of the day to help raise money for the library—people could choose to bid on their own creations or take someone else's home as a centerpiece to their holiday table.

Jenna, however, like most of her family members, would be staffing the event. It was fine; she had years of gingerbread house decorating behind her and she knew from experience that it was more difficult than it looked, especially when it came to piping. Try as she might, her creations rarely (make that never) came out as she envisioned them, and she was yet to get a roof attached without a mess of royal icing to show for it. She was just as content to help where needed and participate in the fun from a distance.

Amelia and Maddie were overseeing things today, as they'd done last year, but after the tree lighting ceremony on Friday, they'd also mentioned they would be donating a gingerbread house for auction—one they would manage to work on in the kitchen while overseeing everyone's dough and making sure that nothing was getting burnt in the industrial ovens. Jenna could only admire them; no doubt there would be a bidding war for their creation.

Now, as Jenna entered the very room where the town meeting had just been held last night, she saw how quickly it had been transformed. The window pass to the kitchen was open, and Candy, like last year, had decorated its frame with lights and garland and a sign boasting her hot chocolate for sale. Usually, the proceeds of this went toward the Winter Carnival decorations, but with everyone donating so much for the carnival already, these proceeds would go straight to the library fund.

"Oh, Jenna, I'm so glad I spotted you." Candy grabbed her by the elbow and pulled her over to the refreshment stand, where, like last year, Candy Cane Hot Chocolate was proudly displayed on the chalkboard menu, pun very much intended. "I wanted to talk to you about the costumes for the choir."

Jenna had been bracing herself for this exchange ever since Candy first hinted at it at their last rehearsal. "I'm not sure that it's in the budget, Candy," she explained, hoping that with everyone pulling together to save the library, this would shut down further conversation. Already she had visions of striped knee socks, joker hats, and other items that one might associate with an elf in Santa's village.

"We're both on the Winter Carnival planning committee this year," Candy said earnestly. Still, it was difficult to take her completely seriously when her not-so miniature

Christmas tree earrings kept blinking like that. "We must make this year's event extra special, so I got to thinking…"

Oh, dear. When Candy got to thinking, things got a little difficult for the rest of the Conway women. This was what led to Candy changing her wedding flowers half a dozen times and her wedding gown possibly more. Both of Jenna's sisters had been on edge for months, only relaxing once Candy began her rather dramatic march down the aisle.

"I think a lot of people like the Winter Carnival just as it is," Jenna said. "Why change it?"

"Oh, there's always room for improvement, even when it comes to Christmas traditions." Candy waggled her finger at Jenna, but Jenna didn't find it funny. Candy had inadvertently hit a nerve, reminding her of Mr. Dunne's similar words.

Well, she had an opportunity to show him, didn't she? The mayor had sent her over a copy of the choir sign-up list this morning, which included a fair percentage of the children in town. Jenna's mind had been buzzing all morning, thinking of how she could put her ideas into action with no financial resources and little time to rehearse.

"All right, then, what did you have in mind?" She braced herself, expecting something loud and over the top, as was Candy's style.

"I was thinking about how Cora does a theme for our Christmas dinner each year," Candy said. "It goes along with her entire theme for her shop window. So we talked about it last night after the town meeting…"

Jenna nodded politely. She could only hope that Cora had advised her in the right direction.

"And Cora just loved my idea!" Candy proclaimed.

Jenna chewed her lip, unsure if this was true. Cora was a gentle soul; perhaps she was being kind. Or perhaps she had run out of energy to argue with Candy. Cora had a boyfriend and his daughter to focus on now, not to mention that it was the busiest time of year for her shop; perhaps she no longer cared so much if Candy was determined to turn their Christmas dinner table into a scene out of Rudolph.

Reindeer. It would possibly be worse than the elves.

"What about an old-fashioned Christmas?" Candy said, clasping her hands together. She blinked expectantly at Jenna, and Jenna, was, surprisingly, at a loss for words.

"That's....that's a *wonderful* idea, Candy!"

And it was. They'd never had a theme for the carnival before, but now she could picture it, downtown Blue Harbor, with its quaint shops and homes and inns, all decked out with wreathes and ivy and red velvet bows, and her choir, caroling door to door, just like they might have done in generations past. She could see her children's choir, standing in the town square as the snow gently fell around them, holding candles and singing "Silent Night"—Mr. Pritchard's favorite carol. It would be beautiful. It would be serene. It would be special.

But it would be expensive. And how could she expect people to donate more when they were trying to save the library?

"Oh, but costumes like that would be a fortune!" She swallowed back her disappointment, kicking herself for allowing herself to feed into Candy's contagious enthusiasm.

"Don't you worry about that. I know a place two towns over. A theatre. I used to be quite the starlet back in my day," Candy added with a lift of her eyebrow. "They said I might have the potential to go all the way." She gave a little sniff and fluffed her blond curls.

Jenna tried to keep her face straight. "Really?"

Candy leaned in. "They said that I was too big for them. I should focus on something like Broadway. Hollywood."

"Of course." Jenna tipped her head, swallowing hard. "And…what do they have to do with the costumes?"

"Oh!" Candy looked momentarily disoriented, as if she'd been reliving her day in small-town musicals. "They put on a Dickens production each year and they have plenty of costumes that we can borrow. They'll lend them to our choir free of charge."

"Free of charge?" Jenna was skeptical. Candy dreamed big, and she didn't back down easily.

Candy hesitated and then slid her eyes to Amelia and away again. "I may have offered them a free cast dinner, compliments of the café. I'm waiting for the right time to tell Amelia."

Jenna laughed. Amelia might act annoyed, but Jenna knew that she wouldn't mind. She loved to cook and feed people, and besides, this might bring in some new regular customers. Jenna wasn't sure that anyone could resist one of her potpies on a cold winter night.

Jenna started to feel excited, thinking that could weave the theme into the decorations, maybe even get some people into the fun of it by having attendees don their more traditional coats and hats and anything else they might find in their old chests. She was sure that Maddie would love to offer some old-fashioned treats, and maybe Britt and Robbie would be willing to make wassail.

"Since we already carol door-to-door on Christmas Eve, why not also carol around the carnival? The costumes would set the tone for the entire event!"

Jenna couldn't agree more. "Please tell them thank you for us. It's a wonderful idea."

"You can thank me later," Candy said with a wink that made Jenna leery. It was clear from the coy way that Candy was looking at her now that her need for payback had nothing to do with the costumes—and everything to do with Scrooge.

Jenna's eyes latched onto Travis Dunne, who was standing near the gingerbread decorating table, giving her a funny look.

"Tell me you didn't assign me to the decorating table," she said flatly to Candy. Normally, doling out gumdrops and licorice would be one of the more coveted volunteer jobs, but today, she'd rather be on clean-up duty.

"Did you see that man?" Candy all but swooned as she fanned her face with her hand. She dropped her voice to a stage whisper and said, "No ring. And I asked around. He's filling in as the principal at the school."

"I'm aware of that," Jenna said drily.

"So you've met him?" Candy looked only slightly disappointed that she hadn't made the introduction.

"Oh, I've met him all right." Jenna began unwinding her scarf. "And you can tell that theatre that if they need an understudy for Scrooge, Ebenezer himself is just a few towns away!"

Candy's mouth dropped but she said nothing more and Jenna began the short but slow walk to the folding table that housed everything from candy canes to marshmallows of all shapes and sizes.

She could feel Travis's eyes on her as she approached, but she refused to look up, knowing that she would probably be met with a gloating smirk.

Instead, she took her position around the table, as far as she could reasonably stand from him, and tied the red-and-white-striped apron around her waist, to signal that she was a volunteer.

"We meet again," he said, forcing her to glance his way.

"It's a small town," she said with a tight smile. "Though I'm surprised that you're involved in this event."

"I happen to be on the Winter Carnival planning committee. Seems that includes volunteering at many of these fundraising events."

There was a long stretch of silence while Jenna absorbed this information. Travis seemed to take pleasure in it, judging from his poor attempt at hiding his smile.

"I didn't think Christmas traditions were your thing." Jenna began straightening the candy dishes, grouping them by color.

"I thought I should probably get involved in the community while I'm here." He shrugged. "And it's for a good cause."

"It's nice to see that you care about some aspects of this town," she said pertly.

"I see that you're still upset about the pageant," he said instead of explaining his presence.

Jenna tightened the strings of her apron and picked up a bag of peppermint candies. They could argue all night long about this, but it wouldn't change a thing.

"The pageant or the music department?" She raised an eyebrow. "You left that part out of our meeting, though now that I look back on the conversation, you did hint at it."

Travis rubbed the spot between his eyebrows. "I'm afraid it's out of my hands. The board makes the decision."

Jenna's hands shook as she opened a bag of marshmallows and filled a bowl. "And what could be more important to the board than giving the children of Blue Harbor a diverse and complete education?"

"A new heating system? That playground equipment has seen better days, too."

Jenna's heart sank when she saw the frankness in his expression. "There must be funds somewhere. And the kids don't have music class every day!"

"No, but it's a cost. The space, the equipment, most of which are rentals, and the salary of the teacher. Something has to go."

"You're making this sound like it's a done deal." When he didn't reply, Jenna set her hands on her hips. "You must have some influence."

"I'm new. And I'm temporary," he reminded her.

Jenna shook her head. "Maybe once the board members see the children's choir, they'll have a change of heart!" Jenna felt momentarily optimistic until she saw the resigned look on Travis's face. He didn't argue with her, but he didn't encourage her, either. "I suppose the decision to cut the pageant didn't help matters."

"You have the children's choir now. That's good, right?"

She narrowed her eyes on him. "Not good enough. Not that I support cutting any arts programs, but may I ask, why music?" When he didn't immediately respond, she pulled in a breath. "Did the fact that each year the pageant was the same have anything to do with it? What was the word you used again? Oh, that's right, stale. Funny that I tend to use the word tradition in its place."

"I'm sorry that you're so upset."

"Darn straight I'm upset!" She took a calming breath, then lowered her voice. "But this happens to be one of my favorite Christmas events of the year and I don't intend to let you spoil it for me too." She blinked rapidly at the candy, knowing her hands were shaking too hard to sort any of it right now.

His expression softened. "I didn't mean any harm. Actually, I was trying to catch up with you last night at the town meeting."

Her heart skipped a beat. Maybe he'd had a change of heart! She smiled up at him, feeling like a heel for giving him such a hard time. Maybe he'd advocate for the department. He of all people had the power, certainly, even if he was just temporary. Without Suzanne, he was her only hope.

Hope. Mr. Pritchard's kind face came to her mind. There was always hope at Christmas.

"Oh?" She held her breath, hoping that he would tell her what she wanted to hear.

"I was very impressed with your performance at the tree lighting ceremony."

She waited to see if there was more, but from the heavy pause, she was disappointed to realize that there wasn't.

"Flattery won't make me forgive you if that's what you're hoping."

She turned back to the plastic bowls and began filling one with colorful sprinkles, only spilling a few.

"I wasn't trying to flatter you." His mouth quirked into a little smile when she slanted him a glance. "That seems to be your territory."

Her eyes narrowed on him but darn it if she didn't feel her cheeks flame. So he *had* heard her conversation with the girls on Friday night, and it didn't appear that anything she might say could get her out of this jam. Besides, she couldn't even think of a plausible explanation. She'd admitted he was good looking, nothing more. She'd also clarified that he was a first-class Scrooge, something that he was confirming with each passing second.

"I try to see the good in people," she said with a lift of her chin. "And as I could find nothing redeeming about your character, I had to settle on your looks."

"Oh, is that what it was?" His eyes gleamed as Jenna's cheeks flamed.

"I think we should get back to discussing the music department."

"I'm afraid there isn't much more to say on the matter. There is only so much funding."

"In case you haven't noticed, everyone in town is fighting to protect the arts by pulling together for the library. Why not music?" But therein lied the answer. There was only so much money, only so many donations. And the townspeople had found their cause.

Tears threatened to fall but she pushed them back, straightening her shoulders. It wasn't even her department. She had her own business giving piano lessons. But that music department was a part of her past and a part of who she was today.

"I understand that you're disappointed about the pageant. If it makes you feel better, the kids are having fun with the class party idea," Travis said. "Mr. Pritchard is using it as an opportunity to introduce different music styles, and the gym teacher is helping them with some dance routines. We have some country music, some techno—"

"Techno?" She gaped at him. "Techno Christmas music?"

Travis shrugged. "Why not?"

"Because...because..." Because of so many things! She stared at him, eyes blazing, and then tossed up her hands. "We need more marshmallows!"

She marched over to the boxes of unopened supplies stacked against the wall, nearly colliding with dear old Mabel Gibney's wheelchair.

"Mrs. Gibney! I'm so sorry, I didn't see you there!" She smiled at the woman and shook her head at her behavior. Few people in town loved Christmas more than Mrs. Gibney, and she always came out for each town event, even as the years made it more difficult for her.

"It's perfectly fine, dear. You seemed to be in a real rush. Running to meet someone?" Her eyes twinkled.

More like running from someone, Jenna thought. But, seeing no need to bog the poor woman down with all her complaints or troubles, she kept the conversation light. It was Christmas after all, and the gingerbread event was special for most members of the town, especially Mrs. Gibney, who still managed to expertly tile a candy roof, despite arthritis in her hands.

"I'm glad I saw you, though, Jenna," Mrs. Gibney said firmly.

From behind the table, Jenna heard Travis clear his throat. Mrs. Gibney frowned deeply at him and then smiled up at Jenna.

"I don't think I could have enjoyed your performance Friday more. You have such a gift!"

Sometimes, a moment like this was all that was needed to remind her to keep going. It wasn't the flattery—no, it was the fact that she'd made a difference to someone, even for one night or a single moment.

"I'm glad you enjoyed it, Mrs. Gibney. I'm afraid that not everyone appreciates our Christmas festivities, and it means a lot that you do."

Mrs. Gibney looked at her sharply. "What do you mean?"

"Unfortunately, the school pageant has been canceled this year." Jenna shrugged at the woman's confused expressions and explained, "The board feels budget cuts are necessary."

"Well." Mrs. Gibney pinched her lips. "That is a shame indeed, but I will be looking most forward to your carols this year. You will still do that?"

"Of course," Jenna reassured her. "Can I get you some gumdrops?" She knew from years past that Mrs. Gibney was a fan of classic colors, and the green and red candies did tend to go quickly.

"Don't let me keep you from where you're going," Mrs. Gibney assured her with a gentle pat on the hand. "My grandson can help me just fine."

Jenna frowned at her. "Grandson?" And then, with knowing dread, she turned to see Travis grinning back at her.

Jenna swallowed hard. "This is your..." She couldn't finish that thought. Couldn't make sense of it.

"My grandson. He's finally come to have a nice long visit with me." Mrs. Gibney waggled her eyebrows and whispered, "Handsome, isn't he? Single, too, in case you were wondering."

Jenna wasn't, but she was too polite to crush the old woman's pride. She gave a withering smile and said, "I need to check on my, um, cousins."

With that, she strode with firm determination into the kitchen where she knew that the only people who would be back there at this time would be Amelia or Maddie.

She found them huddled over a square of gingerbread. Unlike the other participants, their house was not a simple box, but rather a Victorian-style home, complete with a porch.

Mrs. Gibney was Travis's grandmother! How was that even possible?

"I swear, if this wasn't for the library and helping out Helena, I would get my coat and leave right now!"

"What's going on?" Amelia looked at her in alarm, her piping bag still in her hand.

"It seems that Candy has moved on to my love life." Jenna fished a gumdrop from a candy bowl and popped it into her mouth. "She stuck me at the supply table with our new principal!"

Maddie chuckled. "It was bound to happen. And once she's through with you, one of the Clark girls will be next."

Jenna had to agree there. The Clarks, being related to her mother, were not an extension of her father's family, but that didn't stop Candy from treating them as if they were.

"I need a good look at this man." Amelia walked over to the door and glanced through the circular window at the top. "He *is* cute!" Amelia whispered, and then, seeing

Jenna's expression, gave an apologetic grin. "Maddie told me about Friday night."

"Then you also know that he canceled the holiday pageant and, if he has it his way, will also eliminate the entire music program!"

She knew she sounded like she was in denial, but she wasn't willing to believe that the music department could be cut until she heard it directly from Suzanne.

"Why is he talking to Mabel Gibney?" Maddie asked, turning from the window.

"That's what I was about to tell you. She's his grandmother!"

Both cousins stared at her in disbelief, but it was Amelia who spoke first. "I seem to remember that she had a grandson visit her in the summer a few times. We were just kids, caught up in our fun, so I didn't pay it much attention."

"Her daughter never visited though," Maddie remarked. "I remember hearing that she passed away a couple of years back."

Jenna frowned at this. "That's sad." Very sad. But not enough to make her give the man a pass.

Amelia tipped her head. "I know it's disappointing to you that the pageant was canceled, but think of all the time you have to devote to the fundraising efforts. And you have the children's choir now! Maybe it was a blessing in disguise."

"I know," Jenna said, "but he doesn't know that. And he didn't care that he took away something special from me or that…" Shoot. She could feel the tears burn in the

back of her eyes and she blinked quickly, hoping to push them back in their place.

"Something tells me that this is about more than the school pageant," Maddie said softly.

Jenna sniffed, happy that she'd managed to stop her tears before they fell. This was supposed to be a happy day. She would not let that man ruin it for her. "Sometimes I wonder what might have happened if I'd gotten into that music academy." She gave a nonchalant shrug but her heart felt heavy. It wasn't just about wondering what path her life might have taken, it was a bigger question, one that made her wonder not what if but why? Why hadn't she been good enough?

"There wouldn't be a Christmas choir, or all these kids learning piano," Amelia said frankly. She measured out a cup of flour and began sifting it into a large bowl. "Would it make you feel better if I assigned someone else to dish out the candy? You could oversee the auction sign-up sheets instead?"

Jenna nodded. "Thank you."

Amelia gave her a wink of camaraderie. "You're an important part of this community, Jenna. Don't lose sight of that over one outsider."

Jenna swallowed hard, knowing that her cousin was right. Travis was an outsider. He was temporary. And soon, he would be gone.

Normally Jenna gave her students an extra few minutes if she didn't have another lesson directly afterward, but today, she was eager for little Owen to finish his last attempt of "Three Blind Mice." She eyed the clock that was discreetly placed on top of her piano, next to the photo of her with her parents and sisters taken next to the lake one summer.

A knock on the door signaled that Owen's mother had arrived, and Jenna helped him quickly collect his lesson book as she walked him into the hallway.

"Hello!" Jenna was always happy to see Tina Jacobs. She'd been a friend of Gabby's in school, and a frequent visitor at their home growing up, too. "He did wonderful today."

Tina's reaction was not the smile that Jenna had been expecting. "Owen is so crushed not to be able to dress up as a toy soldier this year! And we're all so disappointed we won't be able to enjoy your beautiful music at the pageant this year."

Ah. So word was spreading.

"A class song just isn't the same," Tina continued.

Especially not when you took a dance club take on classic carols, Jenna thought.

"We don't even get costumes, just a Santa hat!" Owen complained as his mother helped him into his coat. "And we don't get to hold one of those battery-operated candles for the final song, either!"

Jenna and Tina exchanged an amused smile. "Well, I'm sure it will be special in its own way." She wasn't sure of that at all, but she wanted Owen to enjoy himself, all the same. "I'm not sure if you've heard that some of the children will be performing at the Winter Carnival?"

Tina looked surprised at this news. "No! Is it too late to sign up?"

Jenna smiled warmly. "Never too late. I'm planning to send out a rehearsal schedule by tomorrow morning. As they say, the show must go on!"

Tina looked visibly relieved. "Oh, I'm so happy to hear this. What's Christmas without a pageant?"

"My thoughts exactly." Jenna ruffled Owen's hair. "Now don't forget to practice the song on page ten and pay attention to your fingering. We'll work on it again next week."

"Yes, Miss Jenna," he said before giving her a big toothless smile. "We're going to decorate our tree tonight!"

"And I'm going to go pick one out!"

Tina reached for the door handle and ushered her son into the stairwell. "You'd better hurry. I drove by the lot on my way here and it looked a little picked over."

Just as Jenna had feared. She closed the door behind the Jacobs family and quickly put on her coat and boots.

Bart's tree lot was not far on foot, and despite the chilly wind, by the time she made it to the end of Main Street, she was practically out of breath from speed-walking the short distance. She sighed in relief when she saw that while the lot was certainly not full of the larger spruces and Douglas firs that might work in her parents' home, many smaller trees would be the perfect size for her apartment.

"Hey, Bart!" She stopped at the trailer trimmed in colored lights where her longtime friend was drinking something steaming from a thermos. From the smell of it, coffee. Bart might sell Christmas trees, but he wasn't exactly a peppermint hot chocolate kind of guy. "I'm glad to see you saved a few trees for me."

"What's Christmas without a tree?" He grinned. "Besides, I'm sure that if I did sell out, your cousin next door would have been sure to find a fake tree for you somewhere in her shop."

"Oh, no. I want the real thing. The smell. The needles. Just no squirrels hiding in the branches," she warned.

Bart laughed. "Now that would be a first. But if you're looking for one, now's the time to buy. They went fast this year. I'll probably still have a few of the outliers through Christmas Eve. There's always somebody who waits until the last minute."

"Well, I'll go look around," Jenna said, noticing that another car had just pulled up.

With a smile, she walked through the snow-covered aisles of the tree lot, stopping every few feet to admire a tree and check the tag. Bart had draped lights from metal poles all around the square of space, and music filtered in from speakers near his hut. She hummed along to one of her favorite carols as she bent to smell a fresh pine. It was the smell of winter. Better: the smell of Christmas.

Nothing could ruin her mood tonight.

Except...

Oh, *no*. Jenna rounded the bend into the next aisle and directly into the path of Travis Dunne.

"This seems to be a pattern," he said with a good-natured grin and one that Jenna didn't match.

"Most people do buy Christmas trees during December, and Bart's is the only place to buy them around here. Though I have to admit I'm surprised to see you buying a tree, given your lack of enthusiasm for traditions."

His expression didn't waver. And he didn't explain himself either. Instead, he said, "And I would have thought someone as passionate about Christmas traditions as you are would have had their tree decorated by the day after Thanksgiving."

Jenna inched her nose higher and said, "Believe it or not, there are many people in town who actually want my services this time of year."

The playful smile dropped from Travis's mouth. "I'm sure there do, and it's probably going to be our loss."

She eyed him carefully, unsure if that was regret she heard in his tone or just a desire to call a truce. Either way, she decided that one was in order. Travis Dunne may have insulted her and rejected her, but she'd bounced back before and she was doing it again.

She reached out to check the needles of a small blue spruce, her personal favorite, and, deeming it healthy enough to last through to New Year's when she planned to take it down, slipped a "sold" tag over the branch to claim it as her own.

"I'm afraid that one's already spoken for," said Bart, coming up the aisle.

"Oh? I didn't see a tag." Jenna searched the branches, wondering if she'd missed something.

"I'm afraid this gentleman here has already paid for it. He was just waiting for me to tie it to his car." Bart gave her the slightest hint of a smile to show what he thought of Travis not taking on that task himself.

Jenna gave him a similar look, one that said "city boy." They all knew the type—Cora had settled down with one—people who came from the big city, looking for an escape or a change of pace. Some couldn't wait to get back to the crowds and noise, and others found that this pace of life was more to their liking.

It was clear to Jenna that Travis didn't fall into that bucket.

"Please, let Jenna have it," Travis said, raising a hand.

Bart glanced from Jenna to Travis. "I have a few like this but a foot taller."

"No, no." Jenna was shaking her head frantically. The last thing she needed was for Travis to think he'd wiped the slate clean with a good gesture. Besides, several other small trees would fit in her tight living room.

None, however, were her favorite spruces.

"I insist." Travis looked at her frankly. "My grandmother will probably want something a bit bigger anyway, and...it's the least I can do." His gaze was so soft that Jenna felt herself waver, against her better judgment.

"Well, thank you," she said gruffly. But there was no way she'd let him pay for it. "I'll settle up my bill at the counter. I'll probably need a delivery service for this too, Bart."

Not only was there no way she would get this tree up her stairs, but she couldn't risk injuring a hand in the process.

"Sure thing, Jenna. Seeing as you're only a few blocks up, I can get it over on my way home. Might be a couple of hours, if that's all right."

Before Jenna could respond, Travis offered, "I can get it to your apartment for you. Seeing as you're only a few blocks up." He grinned, but Bart looked slightly bewildered when he saw that Jenna was far from amused.

"I don't mind bringing it, Jenna, but it will be a while. I have to do some inventory here and then I have a few deliveries out on the edge of town…"

In other words, she'd be doing Bart a favor by letting Travis, the man who had single-handedly tramped on her Christmas traditions, walk her home.

Thinking of Travis's own words, she finally nodded her agreement. Like he'd said, it was the least he could do for her, after all.

*

The tree was heavier than it looked. Travis was grateful that the sky was so dark in this rural town, and that the Christmas lights wrapped around every lamppost probably weren't enough to reveal the beads of sweat that were gathered at his hairline. Despite the freezing temperatures, he was grateful when they paused at an intersection to let a lone car cross so that he could unzip his wool coat and let the cold wind cut through his sweater.

"I'm just up at the next corner," Jenna said.

His shoulders sank in relief until she said, "We can go around the back to access the stairs."

Stairs? He managed to stifle a groan as he grabbed the twine, wishing he'd thought to wear gloves, and hauled the tree over the street and up to the next curb.

"I'm above this shop here," she said, motioning toward a window that was lit up with glitter and soft lights and a wedding gown that looked like something out of a fairy tale. "My sister is a designer," she said, catching his raised eyebrows.

If he wasn't so out of breath, he might have had a witty comeback, but he was too winded by the time she showed him around to the back of the building and flicked on the lights for the stairwell. A very steep set of stairs seemed to go on forever, the only light coming from a sole lightbulb that hung on the small landing near the door.

"I'm the only tenant," Jenna said. "My sister gets the place included in her rent, so I'm sort of subletting off her for the moment. It's not much, but I like it."

Travis hoisted the tree with a grunt and followed her up the narrow stairwell.

She stopped at the top to fish her key from her pocket and opened the door to reveal polished wood floors, high ceilings, and a cozy kitchen just off the front hall. A living room was visible to the left, a piano consuming the large corner near the window, but as Jenna guided them into the space, he saw that the tree would be the perfect size for the bay window at the other end.

"Do you have a tree stand?" He could tell that guy at the tree lot—Bart—found it comical that he needed help tying a tree to the roof of his car, but that was only because he didn't want to mess up and cause an accident on the road.

"Cora gave me this as a housewarming gift when I moved in," Jenna said, pulling one from a stack of boxes that he had no doubt held lights and ornaments.

"Cora?" he took the stand from her and secured the trunk in place. "Sorry, but I'm afraid I don't really know anyone in town yet."

It wasn't uncommon. He was rarely in any town long enough to get close to anyone. But here in Blue Harbor, where everyone knew each other, it wasn't as easy as other places.

"She's my cousin. She owns Harbor Holidays, if you decide you want some ornaments for that tree of yours." Her eyes glimmered.

"Next to the tree lot?" He grinned. "That's my grandmother's favorite shop in town."

"I know. So you've been in?" Jenna sounded so pleased by this that he hated to let her down.

He shook his head. "I've been getting settled, but...I'll bring my grandmother by soon. She'd like that."

"She would." Jenna fell quiet for a moment. "I'm sorry about your mother. I knew that Mrs. Gibney had lost her daughter a couple of years ago—"

He held up a hand, giving her a good-natured grin that he didn't feel, one that he could only hope disguised the real ache in his chest every time he thought of his mother. She'd spent her entire life hopping around from city to city, relationship to relationship, always seeming to chase something she could never find.

"I suppose I didn't mention that I had a relative in town."

"Well, you can't be all bad seeing as you're related to Mabel Gibney." Jenna gave him a little grin. "She happens to be one of my favorite people in Blue Harbor."

Their eyes met for a moment, and he felt a shift in the room. A warmth came over him that had nothing to do with the exertion.

"And from what I've seen, you might be one of hers," he said, watching a blush rise in her cheeks that made her hazel eyes seem even greener than usual.

And for reasons he couldn't explain, he was starting to think that Jenna might be becoming one of his favorite people in this little town too.

*

After Travis finished setting up the tree until it was almost straight, though maybe just slightly crooked, Jenna handed over a glass of wine and took a long sip of hers. It was strange, having a man in her apartment, especially Travis Dunne of all people. But he had done her a favor, and she had been raised with manners. The least she could offer him was a drink.

"Any more suggestions you can give me about the town?" He took an appreciative sip of the drink and wiped his brow. "I'd like to make this a nice Christmas. For my grandmother," he added.

"Don't worry," she chided. "I know better than to think you have any Christmas spirit in you."

She quickly gulped her wine. What was she doing? Flirting with this man? She cleared her throat and moved over near the small sofa that faced the tree. Definitely crooked, but almost charmingly so. Besides, she didn't have the heart to ask him to move it again. There was still sweat glistening near his hairline.

"If you have a sweet tooth, Buttercream Bakery has the best pastries and breakfast items, especially during the holidays. And right beside it is Firefly Café, which is nearly as popular as the Carriage House Inn." She could tell by the glint in his eyes that she might be getting a little too enthusiastic about some of her favorite spots in town. "The Yacht Club is popular, too, and then there's Harrison's. It's more a bar. My sister's husband's family owns it. More of a guys' hangout spot, so probably not the best place to go if you're looking to meet any women."

Her face burned. It had just come out, and she wasn't sure why. She didn't know his relationship status, and she wasn't fishing for it, either. She'd just summarized the place as best she could, and clearly, from the quirk of his mouth, she'd said more than she should.

"Good to know," he said with a little smile.

She hesitated, wondering if he would say more, given that she'd said entirely too much. But he didn't comment further, leaving her now curious as to whether he did have a woman in his life, and if not, was he looking to meet one or not?

She reminded herself that he didn't know her relationship status either. For all he knew there was a wonderful man in her life, although, if there were, he probably would have helped her carry this tree up the stairs to her apartment.

She walked over to the tree and fluffed a few branches. Travis drank his wine like it was water and she realized that the exertion had probably left him thirsty. He'd been surprisingly helpful, and maybe even a little nice. And he was sweet to his grandmother; she had to give him credit where it was due.

"Can I get you another glass?" She motioned to the now empty one resting in his hand and lifted an eyebrow

"No, I should probably get back to the tree lot and rescue my car," he said with a grin. "Bart's probably finished tying up the tree by now and I wouldn't want anyone to swipe it."

She laughed out loud as she carried their glasses into the kitchen. "You think that someone would steal your Christmas tree?"

He gave her a funny look. "Is that so improbable?"

"Yes. I mean, people in Blue Harbor all know each other, and half the residents don't even bother to lock their doors, but..." She tipped her head. "But it's Christmas. It seems to go against the spirit of the season to steal someone's tree."

He shook his head. "Not everywhere."

"And where is everywhere?" she asked, hedging her bets on New York or Chicago.

"Oh, I've most recently been down in Florida, before that, Texas, Virginia, Boston. I move around a lot."

She sipped her drink. Surely work wasn't the reason for his wandering spirit. "How are the Christmas trees in Florida?"

He gave her a knowing grin. "I know better than to blame the climate on why I never have a tree."

"Decorations at least?" She could already guess his answer, but it was fun to see him squirm just the same.

"I don't collect too many possessions. I move around too much."

No place to call home then. Jenna thought of her own few boxes of holiday decorations she had started to collect and was already looking forward to setting out each year.

"All the more reason I should be happy that I ended up staying put," she said.

He glanced at her. "You thought about leaving town?"

She swallowed back the last of her wine, not wanting to get into all of that. "Oh, years back. College stuff, you know."

He seemed to take that excuse without any further question and made his way to the nearby door to fetch his coat from the hook.

"Thanks again," she said, meaning it.

"I just helped set you up. Now the real works begin." He jutted his chin to the boxes in the adjoining room that she was yet to unpack. "Now you have to decorate it."

"Oh, that's the fun part!" She'd planned to trade her wine for hot chocolate and turn on her favorite carols while she strung the lights and hung the ornaments.

Now, though, as she waved to Travis and closed the door behind him, her apartment suddenly felt empty, and she wondered with a strange sensation if she'd actually enjoyed having him here in her home.

She shook her head, laughing at herself, and turned on the *Nutcracker* soundtrack—her favorite version from the London ballet.

She didn't need a guy to fill her home or her heart, and certainly not Travis.

All she'd ever needed was her music, but now, she couldn't help but wonder if it wasn't always going to be enough.

After a long week of lessons and a successful choir rehearsal for both the adults and children, Jenna decided to take Amelia up on her offer and headed over to the Firefly Café on Friday night for dinner. She crossed Main Street and looked across the road to her apartment windows, where her tree sparkled with white lights reflecting off the gold and red ornaments she'd hung on her. It wasn't as full as the tree in her parents' house, but it would get there over the years.

With her hands in her pocket for extra warmth, she walked along the sidewalk toward the path that cut down to the lakefront. Maddie was locking up the bakery when Jenna approached the building. "Oh, Jenna, I'm glad I caught you!"

"I'm about to have dinner next door if you want to join me." Jenna wouldn't mind the company, so long as her cousin didn't try to play matchmaker and talk about Travis too much.

No such luck. "I'm meeting Cole for dinner at the Carriage House tonight or I would. But I thought I should warn you that I saw Candy a while ago and mentioned that she should back off trying to set you up with our new principal because of, well, the pageant."

This was welcome news. Last night at the choir rehearsal, Jenna had started to explain to Candy the reasons behind the pageant being canceled, but there was too much excitement and chaos in the room for them to get into it for long.

"Unfortunately, I'm not sure I got through to her," Maddie said.

Jenna could only laugh. When a handsome man was involved, Candy tended to ignore everything else. "He's not so bad, actually, so I should probably be relieved that Candy hasn't decided to give him a hard time."

"Not so bad?" Maddie regarded with her interest. "Do tell."

"It's nothing. I've just....decided to believe that the decision was the board's and not his and...give him a second chance. In the spirit of Christmas."

"In the spirit of Christmas." Maddie's mouth twisted as she slung her bag higher on her shoulder. "That's very generous of you, Jenna."

"It was that or let my feelings ruin my holiday." Jenna gave a sad smile. "I've been disappointed before."

Maddie's expression went from one of teasing to one of sympathy. "I know, but can I just say that selfishly I'm really happy you didn't get into that music college? I would have missed you too much!"

Jenna grinned. "I would have missed you, too."

She would have missed all of this. Not just the glow of the town during December, but Maddie's new bakery, her sister's new bridal salon, and Britt's upcoming wedding.

Staying in Blue Harbor had once felt like settling, but now, when she thought of her future, she couldn't imagine ever leaving this town or the people in it. Maybe her mother had been right. Maybe things did happen for a reason, even when they felt like a setback.

Waving off Maddie, Jenna walked around the side of the building to the café. Like its sister storefront, Firefly Café was fully decorated from the outside in, and as Jenna approached the front door, she was happy to see the festive wreath secured by a cheerful bow. This year, Amelia had even set up the deck with heated igloos for her more adventurous diners, and she'd added the special touch of lining them with clear lights, so they seemed to glow from within as if they were really made of ice.

All three were occupied by couples, bundled in their coats, a fur blanket wrapped over their legs, no doubt part of Candy's contribution. Either way, with the view of the moon reflecting off the lake, it was perfectly festive.

And perfectly romantic, she couldn't help thinking. Normally, Jenna didn't long for a relationship or wonder too much when someone special would come along, but at Christmastime, when everything was lit up and sparkling, she couldn't help wishing she had someone to share it all with…which was just as well that she was finding extra reasons to stay busy this year.

Jenna pushed through the front door before she got frostbite and was greeted by the sounds of cheerful holiday music, the din of diners' lively conversation, and Amelia's usual Christmas tree, decorated by patrons of her restaurant.

Through the open pass behind the counter, she saw Candy in the kitchen, but it was Amelia who greeted her first, coming through the swing door with two servings of steaming potpie—one of her specialties in winter.

"You're finally taking me up on my offer!" Amelia grinned as she set the two plates down on a nearby table. The diners wasted no time tucking into the dishes, nodding their approval. "Sit anywhere you'd like, but as you can see, we've got a pretty full house."

Jenna considered her options, which were limited, and decided that a spot at the counter would do. There was only one other patron and she'd be able to interact more with Amelia as she came and went to the kitchen. Jenna was used to eating alone, but not in restaurants, and now she was wondering if she should have asked one of her single cousins to join her tonight—but then, it was Friday night. Natalie would be home with her daughter, and Bella was probably still at the bookshop. She hung her coat on one of the hooks near the door and was just reaching for her phone to text Heidi when she felt someone's stare pulling at her attention.

"This seems to be a theme, running into each other."

Jenna's heart sped up when she looked up at Travis, who was sitting at the counter holding a menu. His dark eyes bore a hint of amusement as he grinned at her; no doubt she hadn't been able to hide her surprise.

"It's a small town, and the Firefly Café is one of the best spots there is." She felt suddenly nervous, but she didn't know why. This man was partially responsible for taking away the town's beloved pageant—but he was also surprisingly kind and easy to talk to and more than a little good looking. And after he'd carried her Christmas tree, she couldn't help but feel conflicted. And that...well, that left her unsure of how to proceed.

"I thought I'd take you up on one of your suggestions and try a new place in town. Looks like I made the right choice."

Given that he hadn't ordered yet, she knew that he couldn't be referring to the food. Still, she didn't read too far into his words as she slid onto the stool beside him and closest to the kitchen door. The room was decorated with all things Christmas, if that was what he was referring to, though given his Scrooge-like approach to the holiday, that might not be what he meant at all.

And that only left...

She slowly unraveled her scarf, feeling the heat of his gaze on her. Surely, he couldn't mean he was happy to run into her?

"You aren't having dinner with your grandmother tonight?"

"She's with her knitting club," he explained. "Something to do with socks for the carnival's craft booth. You actually saved me. It's half-priced bottles tonight. Would you maybe like to share a nice red?"

She gave a little smile. "Considering that I grew up in the wine business, I can't exactly say no."

Besides, she didn't want to. It was cold outside and warm inside, and she couldn't remember the last time she'd shared a bottle of wine with anyone other than one of her cousins or sisters, and even that was becoming rare as their lives became busier.

"Wine business?" He waited for her to explain.

She hesitated, knowing that she should probably keep her distance, but taking in his easy smile, she decided to shelve professional issues for one night.

"The orchard has been in my family for generations, and back when my father and his brother took things over, they started making wine and cider." She smiled fondly. "Some of my happiest childhood memories are from harvest time. We even have a festival every year."

He looked impressed. "I'll have to check it out if I'm still in town."

Right. That. Travis's temporary status applied to his personal life, too, and Jenna would be wise to remember that. He was a storm, shaking things up at the moment, but eventually, he'd pass through town.

"Your grandmother never brought you? She usually attends all the events we have at the orchard."

Travis's smile slipped. "I didn't visit much. My mom and I moved around a lot."

"Is that why you still move so much?" She had meant to be conversational, but the tightening of his jaw told her that she had hit a nerve. "Well, your grandmother loves the harvest fest. All the labels are named after one of the Conway women, and I think her personal favorite is the Brooke. Named after my sister."

His grin returned. "Well, then, perhaps I should let you do the honors."

She didn't need to look at the menu to know what kind of wine they should order, or what she would be eating, either, but she suddenly wished for an excuse to hide behind the shield of the menu when Candy burst out of the kitchen, her arms laden with plates that went all the way to her elbows in a way that made Amelia's gasp across the room audible to everyone.

As if balancing six plates on her arms wasn't enough for Candy, her eyes widened on Jenna and her unexpected dinner companion.

Jenna stifled a laugh as Amelia rushed to carefully remove two of the plates from Candy's arms, but Candy barely noticed. She deposited the remaining plates at a table near the faux fireplace she'd installed last year when she'd first started working at the café, her gaze flitting back to Jenna.

"Is that the same woman from the gingerbread event?" Travis leaned in to ask.

Jenna pulled in a breath to settle her nerves, unsure if it was the anticipation of Candy's impending interrogation or the way that Travis sat close enough for her to smell the musk of his skin and feel the heat of his body.

"It's a small town. You see the same faces everywhere you go."

"So I've noticed." His mouth curved into a grin, and Jenna knew then and there that he wasn't talking about Candy anymore.

"Well, don't you two look cozy!"

Jenna closed her eyes. She should have known. Should have taken the lone table in the corner rather than sitting here at the counter, or at least sat two stools down, so it wouldn't like she and Travis were here together.

But now they were here together, on the same schedule. And about to share a bottle of wine.

"Is this a Winter Carnival business meeting or one of a more *personal* nature?" Candy asked brazenly, causing Jenna's cheeks to flame.

Beside her, Jenna thought she heard Travis smother a laugh, and he picked up the menu, lifting it higher. Considering that as part of the planning committee, Candy knew full well that most of the planning was being done via email, and the real work would come when it came to the actual event, Jenna knew she was caught.

"Just two people who happen to be dining in the same restaurant," Jenna managed. She gave Candy a hard stare. If her aunt took the hint, she didn't show it.

"Well, isn't that a happy coincidence?" Candy waggled her eyebrows. "But then, I like to think there is no such thing as coincidences, especially at Christmastime."

"What would you call it then?" Travis asked, and Jenna had to resist elbowing him, knowing that doing so would only excite Candy further.

Instead, she braced herself for it, knowing that Candy, a hopeless romantic, would claim fate was in action. But Candy just gave a knowing smile and said, "Magic!"

Jenna said firmly, "I'll have the bottle of Gabrielle."

She knew that Candy would understand since she was married to her Uncle Dennis. The "Gab Cab" as it was known in the family was a top seller.

Candy gave her a pointed look. "An entire bottle! My, my. Rough day? Or…celebration?" This was unfortunately followed by a less than subtle wink.

Jenna should have known that Candy wouldn't let this go so easily. "It's half-price today so we've decided to share it rather than order separate glasses…" And she was rambling.

Candy had already tuned her out as she slid her gaze to Travis and let it linger there. "And whose tab should I put that on?"

Oh, for Pete's sake!

"Mine," Travis was quick to say, and because Jenna didn't want to drag out any more argument in front of Candy, she didn't protest.

Candy's eyes widened on her and she hurried through the swing door, where a strange squeal seemed to come through the window pass.

"She's my aunt," Jenna said by explanation.

"Really?" Travis looked intrigued. "You certainly know a lot of people in town."

"She just married into the family this past year, but in many ways, it feels like she's always been a part of it. She's certainly made herself at home."

Travis's brow knitted. Another nerve, perhaps?

Jenna motioned to Amelia as she came through the swinging door, only carrying two plates. "And that's my cousin Amelia. She's an excellent cook, by the way. She even won a regional contest for one of her recipes."

"So a sister with a bridal salon—"

"And another sister with a flower shop. You might have seen it on Main Street?"

"The one who's hosting the wreath-decorating event? My grandmother is looking forward to that." He gave a little smile. "I always wondered what it would be like to grow up in a big family. My mother was an only child, and I was too."

"Any cousins on your father's side of the family?"

"My father bailed before I was old enough to remember him," Travis said with a shrug, but there was a shadow of disappointment in his eyes. "I think that's why my mother liked to keep moving. She called it moving forward, but I just called it moving."

"That must have been difficult," she said quietly. "Saying goodbye to people you cared about all the time."

"I learned not to get too close." Travis held her gaze for a moment and then looked away.

Jenna was relieved to see that it was Amelia who was bringing them their bottle of wine and two glasses.

She gave Travis a little smile as she uncorked it. "I don't think we've been properly introduced. Amelia Conway."

"Travis Dunne." He shook her hand. While she poured them each a glass, he said, "I hear you're quite the chef."

"If you like comfort food." But Jenna could tell she was flattered.

"Beats take-out pizza," he said with a grin, prompting Amelia to flick a glance at Jenna. One that said, single, very likely single. Single and now sharing a bottle of wine with her. Jenna wasn't so sure what that made this, but she'd almost say that they were becoming friends.

"Well, I'd better get back before Candy adds too much cheddar to my mac and cheese."

"Is there such a thing as too much cheese in mac and cheese?" Travis joked.

Amelia and Jenna exchanged a glance and then laughed. They both knew that Candy liked to take things a little too far, and believed there could never be too much of a good thing.

"Are you ready to order or should I give you a few?"

"I think I'll take the house special," Travis said, gesturing to the chalkboard in the corner.

Jenna nodded the same, even though Amelia would already know that's what she'd be having. It was one of her favorite dishes on the menu, a tried and true recipe, a winter tradition, so to speak.

"I'm just about to take a batch of potpies out of the oven, so it won't be but a minute."

"It wouldn't be December in Blue Harbor without Amelia's potpie," she said when her cousin walked away.

Travis reached for his glass and held it up in a toast. "I think it's only fair that we toast to the town library."

"Absolutely," Jenna said firmly. She clinked his glass and took a long sip. "I hope that we're able to pull together enough money to keep it open."

"It's a shame to think of losing it," he agreed.

"Is that why you joined the planning committee?"

He nodded, but after a pause. "Something like that. My grandmother likes to be involved, and what she can't do I'd like to do in her place."

Amelia came through the door again with their plates, giving Jenna a wink before she disappeared again.

"Doubt you've had a meal like this in Florida," Jenna said.

Travis looked at the potpie appreciatively. "You could say that again. This feels like a homemade dinner."

Jenna laughed. "Amelia makes everything fresh."

"No, I mean, it feels...like home, you know?"

Jenna did. She just hadn't stopped to think about it that way in a while.

"Man, you weren't wrong about this place," Travis went back for a second bite.

"It's a winter tradition." Jenna picked up her fork happily.

"What is it with you and traditions?"

"Me and this whole town, you could say." Jenna chewed thoughtfully. "You really don't have any Christmas traditions?"

He didn't need to think before answering. "Nope. Unless Chinese take-out classifies as tradition."

Jenna managed a smile. "If you did it every year, then sure."

"Can't say I've kept it up in recent years," Travis replied.

"Well, I don't think your grandmother will let you squirm out of any of her holiday traditions," Jenna said.

"Believe me, I know!" He laughed and took a long sip of wine. "I can't complain much, though. It's nice to be able to keep busy while I'm here with my grandmother and while I'm figuring out what comes next. I went through a breakup last year."

Jenna tried to picture him in a relationship and found that the image came all too easily. Still, she couldn't help wondering why it had ended, and who had been the one to do it.

"I understand the feeling of having all your plans pulled out from under you," she sympathized, even though she didn't have much experience when it came to romance. "It probably happens to everyone in some form."

"If we're lucky, it only happens once," he said with a grin.

She wasn't sure if he meant that he was no longer open to the idea of love, and decided that it didn't matter. She was getting ahead of herself. The man was handsome, surprisingly good company, and as he was quick to point out, only here temporarily. Strange how that no longer thrilled her.

"Well, I'm sure your grandmother is overjoyed to have you with her for Christmas," Jenna said, knowing that Mabel usually relied on the company of her friends around the holidays.

"Actually, I'm in a little trouble with her at the moment." Travis gave her a knowing look and Jenna slapped a hand over her mouth.

"Oh, because of what I said at the gingerbread event?" She couldn't feel too bad, though. She'd just told the truth.

"She'll get over it," Travis said with a shrug. "She sort of has to since I'm her only grandchild."

That was probably true. But did Jenna have to get over it?

"Do you think that anything can be done to save the school arts program?" she asked carefully. She couldn't let the opportunity to advocate for the program slip away, not when Travis seemed to be willing to hear her out.

"If you have any ideas, I'm all ears," he said. Then, setting down his fork, he said, "I meant it when I said that it wasn't personal, Jenna. I hope you believe me."

She nodded, reflecting on his words, seeing the sincerity in his eyes. "I do now. Still, it's hard not to take things personally when it comes to my music."

"You really love what you do."

She thought about this for a moment, knowing that she did, and she didn't just mean in the sense that she enjoyed being able to play the piano every day, or lead the choir. "I enjoy teaching the next generation to appreciate the instrument. There's nothing more exciting than a kid with potential. Watching their progress…I feel honored to play a role in it."

"I feel the same way. It's why I went into education." He was thoughtful for a moment. "My dad wasn't in my life and my mom was working a lot. Some teachers really shaped me. School was a place where I felt safe, and challenged, and where I felt like people were looking out for me."

"That's how I feel about Blue Harbor," Jenna said. "Well, other than the challenging part. Sometimes I can't help but wonder if I took the easy path, staying in my hometown instead of moving on to a bigger city or trying something new."

"Nothing wrong with the tried and true." Catching her look, he grimaced. "I apologize for calling the pageant stale. I have never even seen the school's previous pageants."

"And yet you were eager to change it." The sting had returned.

"I was trying to make the best of a bad situation." He looked at her frankly. "If there was a way to turn it around, I would. For what it's worth, a lot of people are disappointed. I've had calls from a lot of upset parents."

Jenna couldn't help but perk up a bit, but it was short-lived. "That doesn't make me feel any better. I want everyone to be happy. This isn't just about me. It's about something the community values. I just hope the kids still have fun."

Travis nodded. "Me too."

And she could see by the look in his eyes that he meant it.

"I should probably go," Jenna said, pushing her empty plate away. "I have an early lesson tomorrow, before school."

"Well, this was nice, Jenna. Maybe I'll see you around again sometime."

She gave a little smile as she wrapped her scarf around her neck. This was Blue Harbor. And it was Christmastime, meaning everyone was out and about.

He could count on it.

Jenna had to hand it to Candy. By ten o'clock the next morning, Main Street was alive with shoppers eager to partake in the first annual Christmas Stroll. Jenna watched from her living room window as families and couples and friends walked slowly down the snowy sidewalk, most holding red shopping bags, all in good spirits.

She pulled her gift list from the coffee table and skimmed it once more, making sure that she hadn't missed anyone. Her family was growing with each passing month, it seemed, and she liked to give something small to each of her students, too. This year, she would get them each a small ornament unique to their personalities. But first, she wanted to stop by the bookstore and get a new cookbook for Amelia, who was always looking for inspiration from her favorite celebrity chefs.

Just thinking of Amelia made her think of the Firefly Café. Last night had been strange, unexpected, and surprisingly fun. She'd smiled for the entire walk home, which she'd taken alone, even though Travis had offered to drive her. She'd passed on that—she had to draw the line somewhere, otherwise, she risked making the whole night feel like more than it was or should be. Travis had been surprisingly easy company, once the sensitive topics were shelved.

Sometimes, she supposed, it took having dinner with a stranger to make you realize how much nicer it was to share a meal.

Brooke was in her shop when Jenna came downstairs, armed with her list, her credit card, and careful layering so that she could withstand a long day. Usually, she would have waited to go shopping with her sisters, but as they each ran a shop in town, they were eager to participate in today's fundraising efforts, and Jenna was just as excited to support it. If she could manage to fit all of her Christmas shopping into this single day, she'd end up donating a considerable sum to the library, not to mention be exhausted enough to warrant a hot bath followed by flannel pajamas, and a quiet evening with her favorite Christmas movie.

Normally this type of thing would be something she'd look forward to, even if her sisters would chide her about it, claiming she needed to get out more. Now, after last night, it felt a little less exciting than it would have just a week ago…and a little lonelier too.

"You look ready for the day." Brooke was changing out the floral arrangements, swapping the red roses with soft greenery, winter berries, and creamy roses. "You just missed Gabby, though. She dropped these off. Aren't they lovely?"

"Pretty enough to make me certain that if I ever get married, it will be at Christmastime," Jenna remarked, admiring the oversized bouquet on the center table.

"If you ever get married?" Brooke tsked her disapproval. "You're young and pretty. You can't stay holed up in that apartment playing the piano or listening to classical music for the rest of your life." She stopped fluffing the greenery to give Jenna a pointed look. "You forget that when my shop closes, I often stay late in the backroom sewing. I know your routine. I know that you spend way too much time at home, alone."

"There's nothing wrong with being a homebody," Jenna said defensively.

"There's nothing wrong with getting out once in a while, either."

"Well, I'm on my way out, now, and if you keep this up much longer you might end up with a lump of coal from me instead of what I originally had in mind."

Brooke grinned. "Point taken."

"Do you think you'll get many customers stopping in today?" Jenna asked, wondering if most people would be sticking to Christmas gifts instead of wedding gowns or accessories.

"I put out a notice on all my social media accounts," Brooke said, nodding. "If someone's in the market for an off-the-rack wedding dress or accessories, today is the day to stop by! Ten percent discount, which is a fair amount considering the price tag."

"That's very generous of you." Jenna knew just how expensive a wedding gown could be, even if she'd had no personal experience.

Brooke tidied her desk in the corner of the showroom. "We're all just doing our part. I see it as a win-win for everyone in this town. Shops will see a big increase in sales and with a portion of the proceeds going to the library, we're also helping a worthy cause."

Jenna nodded. "I should do my part and start shopping, then."

"You're already doing your part," Brooke said with a smile. "You have the choirs, and Candy mentioned you're on the Winter Carnival planning committee with her. You seemed to be working pretty hard at the gingerbread event, although I heard that you and our new principal had to be separated."

Despite herself, Jenna burst out laughing. "You make it sound like we're a pair of children."

"Two attractive adults of the right age is more like it." Brooke gave a dramatic sigh as she finished tweaking the flower arrangement. "If only you could find a way to get along."

Jenna wasn't about to take the bait. "Travis is...well, he's not such a bad guy after all."

Brooke let her fingers drop from the vase. "Travis, is it? Here I thought it was Mr. Dunne. Or was it...Scrooge?"

Jenna laughed and adjusted her tote bag on her shoulder. "He certainly doesn't have much Christmas spirit."

Still, she supposed that there was a reason for it, even if it was perhaps a choice by now.

"If I didn't know better, I'd say you were starting to thaw toward him." Brooke gave her a little smile.

Thinking back on Travis's comments about not getting too close to people, Jenna shook her head and moved toward the door. "Look outside. Even the snow isn't thawing." And neither, she gathered, was Travis's frozen heart.

*

Bella's Books glowed from within the large bay window and paned glass door. In her planter, she'd placed a small Christmas tree, complete with lights and a star-shaped topper. Jenna pushed through the door and breathed in the scent of a pine candle and paper. The store was crowded, as it often was, but Isabella still made her way over to Jenna with a smile.

"I was beginning to think I'd never recognize a face in here today!"

"That many tourists?" Jenna looked around the store, not seeing anyone she knew. Except…

Her heart sped up at the sight of Travis engrossed in the jacket copy of a new thriller. She looked away and wondered fleetingly if she should leave now, come back later, or say hello. Or wait to see if he said hello.

Last night had been nice, but it also left her unsure of where they stood. Was she still mad at him? Were they friends?

Friendly, she decided. Maybe, even friendly enough to make him have a talk with the board about the music department.

"I'm expecting more locals here soon. Storytime is starting in thirty minutes and we have a special guest doing today's reading."

Jenna was just about to ask who that might be when the question was answered for her. The door jangled as a gust of sharp cold air pulled her attention and there stood her Uncle Dennis and Aunt Candy. Or rather, Santa and Mrs. Clause.

"I thought that the Davidsons were playing Santa again this year!" she stage whispered to Bella, in case any children were in earshot.

Bella shook her head. "Mr. Davidson hurt his knee and can't handle any kids jumping onto his lap. And of course, Candy was all too happy to volunteer!"

Jenna wondered how her Uncle Dennis felt about being tucked into a red velvet suit and white beard, but his eyes shone as he let out a merry "Ho, ho, ho!" and slowly made his way to the children's corner, nearly crashing into two display tables from his fake girth.

Behind him, Candy handed out candy canes to each person she passed, stopping when she found Jenna and Bella. "What do you think?" She blinked rapidly. "Too much?"

If by too much, Candy was referring to three-inch candy cane earrings that flashed red and white, or the matching necklace that circled her neck, Jenna could only laugh.

"Can there ever be too much Christmas?" she asked.

Candy beamed and ran a hand over the velvet dress, which, like most of Candy's clothing, hugged her curves.

Jenna supposed that if there was any intention of slipping out of the shop without Travis seeing her, that opportunity had closed. Between Candy's flashing jewelry and large bouncy curls, she had caught the eye of nearly every person in the store.

Sure enough, as she moved toward the cookbook section, she caught Travis smiling at her from the display table. He set down the book and walked over to where she stood. "Here I thought maybe you were about to get into an elf costume and join them."

"Please don't speak too loudly," she teased. "We don't need Candy getting any more ideas."

"You have to admit her ideas are good ones, though," Travis said, and Jenna couldn't argue. Candy had pioneered the library fundraiser; Jenna could only hope that a project this large would keep her aunt's mind off her current love life.

She glanced at Travis. Not that she had one, or needed one.

Travis jutted his chin to the display of cookbooks. "Christmas cookies. That's sort of a thing, right?"

She choked down a laugh and looked at him strangely. He hadn't been exaggerating when he said he never partook in Christmas traditions, however small. "You're joking, right?"

He picked up the book and flipped through some of the pages. The photographs were appealing enough to make Jenna consider buying the book for herself, especially knowing that it would benefit a worthy cause.

"I'm here to buy a gift for my cousin Amelia," she said, lifting the newest book from one of Amelia's favorite chefs from a table. "But yes, I think I might buy this one, too." She motioned to the book he was still holding. "I do happen to bake Christmas cookies. My sisters and cousins all do a swap each year."

"A swap?" He looked intrigued.

"A cookie swap." Boy, he really didn't know much about Christmas, did he? "It's an excuse for a holiday party. Everyone brings what they bake and then we can all bring a box home."

"Sounds delicious," Travis said.

Jenna looked at him as she took the book from his hands. "You've never baked Christmas cookies?"

"My mom was a single parent and she worked long hours. But sometimes our Chinese take-out came with a fortune cookie." He grinned, but there was a sadness in his eyes that told her maybe he had missed out on more than a traditional meal.

"I'd love to know what you gleaned about your future," she said diplomatically as they moved toward the counter. "Did the cookies ever tell you that you'd end up in this snowy little town for the best Christmas ever someday?"

He held her gaze for a long moment. "I sort of wish it had."

Startled, Jenna frowned at him, then turned to face her cousin at the sound of a throat clearing. Bella stood behind the old-fashioned cash register, looking at Travis with open interest, and Jenna saw no way around an introduction. "Bella, this is Travis. Travis, my cousin Bella."

He gave her a funny look. "You certainly have a lot of cousins."

"Big family, and Bella's on my mother's side." Jenna grinned at Bella, but Bella was too busy shaking Travis's hand to notice. She paid for the books while dodging Bella's curious glances, thankful that Candy had broken into song in the children's room, which was making Bella twitch.

"I thought she would save it for caroling," Bella whispered with a pleading look.

"I never thought it possible, but I do believe that she enjoys Christmas music even more than I do." Jenna laughed as she took her shopping bag from her cousin and moved toward the door, Travis still beside her.

She wondered if they would politely part on the snowy sidewalk, but instead, Travis looked at her and motioned to the kiosk parked at the end of the block. "Can I buy you a hot chocolate, or do you have a lot of shopping to do?"

Jenna couldn't fight her smile. "I do have a lot of shopping, but I won't turn down a hot chocolate."

He grinned. "Good, because I have a lot of shopping, too, and I'm sort of procrastinating."

"Oh?" She glanced at him as they moved toward a beverage stand that had been set up just for today, sponsored by one of the local restaurants.

"I have a special lady in my life and it's important that I don't mess up the gift."

Oh. Jenna didn't know why but she struggled to keep her smile and look him in the eye at the same time. Instead, she focused on the hot cocoa that was steaming from its warm pot, a sharp contrast to the cold air. When he'd said that he moved on account of a bad breakup, she hadn't considered that he had moved on to someone else.

Travis placed their orders and handed her a cup. "My grandmother can be a little…blunt."

Jenna laughed loudly, happy that she hadn't yet taken a sip of the hot drink. No doubt she would have choked on that remark. His grandmother! Of course! Really, though, she wasn't so sure why she was nearly giddy with relief.

"Your grandmother is a wonderful lady," Jenna said, even though she had to agree with his assessment. Once, while caroling, Mabel had cut them off during the first song and asked them to sing something else instead. Ever since, they'd stuck with her preferred playlist.

"Wonderful, but picky. I don't want to disappoint her."

"Think about what she likes to do, what her hobbies are. I know she loves to craft and knit. And if all else fails, buy her some nice Christmas decorations. I'm headed over to Harbor Holidays to get some things for my students."

"That's a good idea," he said, seeming buoyed by the idea.

"But first..." Jenna grinned as she studied the toppings that had been set up for the hot chocolate. Crushed candy canes, chocolate shavings, sprinkles, and of course, whipped cream. She reached for the cream but then glanced at him sidelong. "Just so we're clear, I'm going to put all of this on my hot chocolate and ask that you reserve judgment."

"Hey, it's Christmas. The time to indulge, right?"

She liked that answer. "It's the time for many things, but yes, indulging is certainly one of them." Their eyes locked for a brief second, and Jenna felt her cheeks heat despite the chill in the air.

"So what do you do with the box of cookies that you take home from your swap party?" he asked as they approached the crosswalk. The walk sign was flashing and Jenna thought they could make a run for it, but Travis pulled her back just in time as a sedan pushed through a yellow light, spraying up an icy puddle onto the sidewalk.

"Thanks," she whispered, feeling her heart pound in her chest, even though she wasn't quite sure if it was from that near brush or the fact that Travis was still holding her arm, even though her safety was no longer in question.

"Some people can be real jerks," he muttered, and she had to resist showing her smile because not so long ago, she had pegged him as one of them.

"They can, but most people around here aren't," she said when they started across the street, clutching their steaming mugs. "And to answer your question, I share my cookies. Christmas is the time for giving, after all."

"Who do you share them with?" He had a funny look on his face as they walked toward the Christmas shop down on the corner.

"My students," she said matter-of-factly.

Travis looked pleased with her response. "Well, that's very nice of you."

"I'm a nice person," she said with a shrug. "Which is why I'm going to help you pick out something for your grandmother. She's a nice woman, too."

"She is," Travis agreed. "Opinionated, but nice." He grinned to show that he was half-joking. "And Christmas is her favorite holiday."

Jenna glanced at him. "Funny that it's your least."

He didn't argue with her. "We didn't spend them the same way. I'm afraid her traditions never made their way down to me."

"Well, it's never too late," Jenna said. "Besides, this is Blue Harbor. In case you hadn't noticed, it's a little hard to ignore Christmas around here."

"Oh, I've noticed." He opened the door to Harbor Holidays and the jingle bells chimed their entrance, underscoring her point.

"Wow." He stopped and took in the scene, which was definitely Christmas at its finest and largest. For years, everyone had been suggesting that Cora cut back on some of her purchasing decisions, at least until she sold more of her current inventory, but she couldn't help herself. Each year she rearranged the store, creating new window displays and themes, adding to her collections of nutcrackers and Santas and villages and reindeer and elves and everything else one could possibly associate with the season.

"Here, let's start at the back. I bet your grandmother would love a new set of ornaments or a topper for her tree?"

Travis nodded and followed her through the winding rooms of the store, each packed to the ceiling with decorations, all smelling of pine or cinnamon, and all filled with the wonderful sounds of holiday music.

She handed him a basket and took one for herself. Little Keira was aching for a dog for Christmas, so she selected a sweet little puppy-shaped ornament for her. Georgie loved skating more than piano, which was fine, even if she didn't exactly practice as often as she could, so Jenna added a pair of skate ornaments to her bag. By the time she accounted for all but three of her students, she looked over to see Travis staring blankly at a snowman-themed tree. His basket was empty.

"Here," she said, motioning him over to a display of household gifts ranging from mugs and oven mitts to candlesticks and platters. She picked up a crimson red picture frame edged in gold leaf. "You could find a special photo and put it in here."

He looked thoughtfully at the frame, which Jenna could imagine his grandmother putting out year after year, perhaps on the mantle, or on a side table near the tree.

"You don't think it's too simple?"

"No, I think it's sentimental. I think it would show how much you care."

He pulled in a deep breath. "I'm afraid I wouldn't even know what kind of photo to put in here."

"Take it. You might surprise yourself. Besides, don't you think it would mean more to her than this platter?" She motioned to an oval platter painted with Santa's jolly face.

He laughed. "Point taken."

Cora, who had snuck up on them, was not so amused. "I happen to like that platter, I'll have you know." She set her hands on her hips, but it was clear by the sheen in her eyes that she, too, had opinions on the piece.

"Cora, this is Travis Dunne, the new principal at the school." Jenna watched as Cora's eyes widened in surprise.

"Temporary principal," Travis corrected, extending his hand. "Is this your shop? It's certainly festive."

"Christmas is my middle name," Cora said. "Or, it should have been. Has a nice ring to it, don't you think?"

"Don't let Candy hear you say that or it will become your new nickname," Jenna warned.

"Good point." Cora eyed their baskets. "All set? We have cookies and hot chocolate in the back of the store, if they aren't all gone by now. I've had more people come through today than any other year."

Jenna was pleased to hear this. It meant the fundraising efforts were working, that by pulling together they actually stood a chance at saving the library. She knew she should be thrilled by this, buoyed by the community spirit and her part in it. Instead, she couldn't help but think how wonderful it would have been if the same people who supported the library could support the music program at the school. She considered asking Travis to name the board members but then decided against it. She was having a nice day, and she didn't want to spoil it. After the holidays, there might still be time to work on the music department, even if it was too late for the pageant.

"We just had hot chocolate, and I still have a lot of shopping ahead of me. Can't afford a sugar crash."

"I'm all set. I only had one person to buy for, but that's more than in past years." Travis didn't look as disturbed by this as Jenna felt. No one else to buy for, meaning no one else in his life? Between her sisters, parents, cousins, and aunts and uncles, not to mention friends, students, parents, and choir members, her life was full, even if her evenings were often spent alone.

But Travis...Wasn't he lonely? Or alone by choice?

"What's this?" When they reached the counter, Travis picked up the snow globe that had been in Cora's family for generations.

"It's a wishing ball," Cora told him. "I gave it to my stepmother, Candy, last year for Christmas, but after her wish came true, she insisted that I keep it here." She looked up in alarm at the sound of a crash. "Uh-oh. Nutcracker down." Cora hurried around the counter and toward a display of Nutcrackers in every shape and size, the largest of which had now tipped into one of the nearest fully decorated trees.

"You think it works?" Travis looked skeptical.

Jenna shrugged. She didn't believe in magic, but she did believe in Christmas miracles. "it's nice to think that it does. It's all part of the feeling of Christmas. It's above all a time for hope, and if something special is going to happen, then it's probably most likely to happen at Christmas."

"And what is your Christmas wish, Jenna?" he asked.

She gave him a knowing look. If he didn't already know, she wasn't about to say it aloud and ruin what had, so far, been another nice day in his company.

She might have her students, and the choir, and all the wonderful festivities that the town offered, but there was a part of her Christmas that was still missing. And she'd be best to remember who was responsible for that.

The Carriage House Inn was one of the most beloved buildings in town, located on Main Street, just a short walk to the lake, with one of the best regional pubs located at the back. It was also owned and operated by longtime family friends of the Conways; the Bradfords were ingrained in this community just as much as the Conways, and it was no surprise that they were showing their support by hosting the gift-wrapping fundraiser in their front lobby.

Jenna arrived with her cousin Heidi Clark, who was the only family member she had that didn't own or work in one of the shops in town, though she wouldn't be entirely surprised if Candy found a way to fit the event into her schedule. Often, Amelia was just as happy to send her stepmother on a break as she was to have her help in the kitchen.

The lobby furniture had been rearranged, giving space for a long table where several people already sat, carefully cutting printed wrapping paper or curling ribbon. Robbie's mother was hosting the event, but she was so busy overseeing the table of volunteers and doling out supplies, that it took a moment before she noticed Jenna.

"Hey!" Bonnie Bradford's cheeks were flushed as she came around the table. "I'm happy you girls stopped by."

"Wouldn't miss it," Jenna replied, even though in years past she had done just that with many of the town events, even when there were far less than this year. The children's choir was a small production compared to the school show, one that would consist of three simple songs compared to a kindergarten through high school event that required more rehearsal time, including from her. How many nights would she sit at the piano, practicing the songs she already knew by heart?

Too many, perhaps, she thought, looking around. She had to admit that it was nice to participate in the other seasonal events for a change. Not that she'd be admitting that to Travis…

And not that she'd be spending much more time with him, either. Yesterday had been a meeting by chance. The other times, too. It was a small town, as she'd told him. It happened.

Now, though, she couldn't help but wonder when it would happen again.

"You have to admit that Candy can be brilliant at times. Expanding the Winter Carnival to a month of festivities has brought a lot of activity to the town," Heidi said. "It not only gave the shop owners a bit of a boost yesterday, but with all the sales from the shopping event, people will have tons of gifts in need of wrapping."

"It was also generous of Cora to donate so much paper and ribbon," Bonnie nodded to show her appreciation. "I offered to pay her, but she wholeheartedly refused, saying I was doing my part by hosting everyone today."

The cousins exchanged a secret smile. They both knew that Cora probably had more rolls of wrapping paper stashed away in the storage rooms of that shop than she'd ever be able to sell, especially when she was constantly adding to her stockpile. She'd never met a new pattern or plaid she could resist.

"Let's grab the two seats at the end." Jenna quickly moved around the table and draped her coat over the back of the chair before she sat down. Soon, they were so engrossed in the task of cutting, folding, and taping, that Jenna barely had time to look up, and when she did, she was surprised to see how much the room had filled.

"Oh, there's Mr. Pritchard!" She held up a hand until she caught his attention. "Is there a gift I can wrap for you?"

He nodded as he approached the table and held out a single box. "I don't have many people to buy for these days, but I wanted to do my part yesterday by buying something. It's for my vet. She's been so good to my little terrier. It's a treat jar to keep on the counter in her office."

"I'm sure she'll love it," Jenna smiled as she centered the box on a large square of paper and began quickly wrapping it. She glanced up at Mr. Pritchard as she reached for the tape, noticing something wary in his eyes, maybe even a little lost. Hoping that she wasn't overstepping, she said, "You know, we can probably use more help. There's a lot of people waiting to get their presents wrapped, and I'm guessing some of the people here will want to take a break soon."

"Oh…" Mr. Pritchard looked around the room with uncertainty, but there was a little curve to his mouth. "As long as you don't expect me to make any of those fancy bows?"

Jenna laughed. "I'll get you a chair." She handed him his wrapped gift and then stood to search for a chair, surprised when she saw Travis and his grandmother pushing through the crowd.

"Travis!" She caught herself. Her tone was considerably more cheerful than she'd intended. He wasn't completely off the hook just yet.

He grinned when his eyes landed on her, but it was his grandmother who positively beamed.

"Jenna Conway!" She looked up from her wheelchair to give her grandson an extremely pointed look. "I'm so happy to see you again, dear."

Jenna didn't read too much into it; no doubt Travis's grandmother was just another well-intentioned, if not entirely off-base, matchmaker, not unlike her aunt—

"Candy!" Jenna looked up to see none other than Candy poking her head over Travis's shoulder, her waggling eyebrows forcing Jenna to let out a sigh as she watched her aunt push through the crowd, grinning very broadly at Travis in the process.

Candy was holding at least a dozen shopping bags—barely holding them, was more like it. She glanced to her aunt's companion, who was taking her time coming through the door, feeling a wash of relief. "And Mom!"

"Hello, honey," her mother said warmly. "Are you helping out today?"

"I am, and given how many people have shown up to have their gifts wrapped, I'm glad I did." Jenna glanced to the side to see Travis maneuver his grandmother's wheelchair away from the crowd that was coming and going through the door.

"Oh, I would have helped out myself but I only have an hour break before I have to get back to the café. We're staying open later today on account of all the activity in town." Candy pouted. "Do you think that's enough time to get all these wrapped?"

Jenna eyed the bulging paper bags doubtfully, but Travis's grandmother cut in before she could reply.

"I can help! Put me to work!"

"Are you sure that's a good idea?" Travis gave her a worried glance, but she swatted him away.

"This grandson of mine won't stop worrying about me even though I've been on my own for most of my adult life. I'm perfectly capable of wrapping a few gifts and tying a few bows. And you'd better roll up your sleeves, too." She gave him a stern look but Jenna could see the twinkle in her eyes.

Travis shrugged and looked at Jenna with a nervous smile. "Guess that means we're volunteering."

"Great." Jenna felt a little breathless as she took the shopping bags from Candy and handed a few to Heidi. There was an awkward moment of shuffling at the table, with a few of the ladies having to move down to make room for the newcomers, and Candy standing guard, clutching the rest of her packages, and double-checking that no surprises would be ruined.

"I'll wrap your gifts myself at home," she told Jenna, Heidi, and Jenna's mother.

"Mr. Pritchard, do you know Mrs. Gibney?" Jenna asked the old man, who was quickly getting the hang of things.

His cheeks turned a little pink. "I certainly do. It's nice to see you again, Mabel."

Mabel giggled like a schoolgirl, and Jenna and Travis exchanged an alarmed glance over their heads which evolved into a slow smile.

"You two know each other?" Travis seemed surprised, and Jenna refrained from pointing out that in a town as small as Blue Harbor, all the locals knew each other. Instead, she waited for the response, interested in just how well these two were acquainted.

"We went to school together," Mabel said.

"I sat behind her every single day for twelve years," Mr. Pritchard said with a mischievous grin.

"So you could pull my hair." Mabel gave him a look of disapproval, even though she smiled as she said it.

"Only up until age ten," Mr. Pritchard said in his defense. "After that, I just admired it. You always did have the prettiest auburn hair I ever did see. If you don't mind me saying."

Now Jenna watched as Mabel's cheeks turned rosy. She gave a little sniff as she reached for a tape dispenser and said coyly, "I don't mind you saying so at all. Just not sure what took you so long."

Jenna looked at Travis and covered her mouth to hide her smile. She was just about to suggest that Travis move to the door as a greeter to maybe give the old sweethearts a little space when Travis's grandmother looked up at her.

"You know what's missing from this event? Music. Here we are, wrapping Christmas presents, and there's no music in the background to make it feel festive."

Jenna couldn't believe she hadn't noticed this first, but with all the buzz in the room, and, admittedly, Travis's arrival, she was a little distracted.

"I can go ask one of the Bradfords to turn on the stereo," she started to say, but Mabel shook her head.

"I see a perfectly good grand piano right there near the window." Mabel jutted her chin toward it, and Jenna tensed.

"Oh, I'd love to hear you play," Mr. Pritchard said. He glanced at Mabel and Travis. "She was my prize student."

Now it was Jenna's turn to blush. "Oh, I'm sure you've had many gifted students in your long career."

"I have had a few," he said thoughtfully, "but you were special, dear."

Jenna looked down at the bow she was tying, taking the compliment to heart, as it was intended. When she hadn't gotten into the music college, she'd always felt like she let two people down: herself, and Mr. Pritchard. Now, glancing up to see the pride in his eyes, she dared to think that hadn't been the case.

"Then you must play," Travis said, holding her gaze.

Before she could think of an excuse (because saying her gift-wrapping services were needed when they had so many volunteers probably wouldn't hold up) a few other people looked up and nodded their agreement.

"Play something for us, Jenna!" Candy called out, sparking a rise of enthusiasm from the crowd.

"I haven't prepared anything. I…don't have my music sheets."

"Pshaw." Candy wasn't buying her excuses. "I see you at rehearsals. You have everything memorized!"

Jenna felt her cheeks burn and she shook her head. "I'm here to focus on the wrapping paper."

"I know! We can do a duet!" Candy blinked hopefully.

Jenna's mother cut a glance to Jenna before gracefully setting a hand on her new sister-in-law's wrist. "You're so good at the bows, though, Candy. I don't think anyone else in this room has your skill set. Maybe you could show a few of us your trick before you have to get back to the café?"

Candy beamed, instantly distracted, but unfortunately, Jenna wasn't off the hook just yet.

"I for one could use a little Christmas cheer if I'm going to sit here all afternoon," Travis's grandmother huffed, even though it was clear from the way her fingers quickly moved to the pile of snowberries that she tucked into a forest green velvet ribbon that she was enjoying herself.

"Me too," Mr. Pritchard chimed in, giving her a pleading look.

Aw, shucks. There was no way she could turn him down and he knew it.

Jenna looked around at the sea of faces and, begrudgingly, pushed back her chair. The piano was in the corner of the room, near the window, with a snowy view of Main Street in all its Christmas glory. She reminded herself that this room was filled with old friends who wouldn't mind if she missed a note.

She glanced at Travis as she sat down at the bench. Even some new friends.

She started with the simple classics—adding a little flourish at the end as she eased into the music, eventually forgetting that she was sitting in the lobby of the Carriage House Inn instead of her cozy little apartment, as she moved effortlessly from one song to the next, transitioning with notes that her fingers found, without having to give much thought or pause.

By the time she finished, the room was hush, and everyone was staring at her.

She froze for a moment, wondering if she'd gone on too long, but then, a cheer went up. She couldn't be sure who led it, but her eyes met her mother's, who was beaming with pride, and then, because she couldn't quite resist, she glanced at Travis, who was grinning ear-to-ear, and, if she didn't know better, clapping the loudest. And given that Candy was attempting to wolf-whistle, that certainly said something.

It said a lot, actually, she thought as she stood and tucked in the bench, her heart swelling with a mix of emotions that she hadn't felt in quite some time, and maybe, she thought, glancing at Travis again, never had before this Christmas.

*

Jenna couldn't have been more relieved when Travis suggested they grab a drink—even if she might have appreciated it if Heidi had tagged along rather than said something vague about going over to her sister's bookstore for a bit.

The gift-wrapping event had been a huge success, and not just for the fundraising effort. Mr. Pritchard and Travis's grandmother were engrossed in a cozy dinner near the fireplace at this very moment, and Jenna supposed that Travis wouldn't be leaving until they were through with their meal. Not that she was in any rush.

The pub at the Carriage House Inn was dark and cozy, with a long, polished wood bar and clusters of tables with black Windsor chairs. For the holidays, it had been decorated with garland and lights, large wreaths on the open doors, and centerpieces made from greenery and pillar candles, no doubt Gabby's creations.

Perched on a barstool, with a mug of hot cider warming her hands and the snow falling gently against the windows to her right, Jenna listened to the soft sounds of the Christmas music that was barely audible over the din of the dining room and thought about how much nicer this was than sitting home alone in her flannels watching a holiday movie—which she'd still do, of course, just later.

"My grandmother is full of surprises," Travis remarked, glancing over his shoulder.

Jenna sipped her hot drink. "I'll say. I still can't believe she persuaded me into performing for everyone today."

"She doesn't back down easily." Travis laughed. "Besides, it didn't seem to bother you too much."

"I'm not used to playing in public," she admitted. She still couldn't believe she'd even done that, and only Candy's insistence had given her the nudge.

"But you played at the tree lighting ceremony," he said.

She nodded. "Yes, but that's different, somehow. That's…rehearsed. And it's only one time a year. And everyone's attention is on the tree. And there are singers, same with the pageant," she added. And the choir. And the weddings she played at, where all eyes were on the bride, as they should be. She had fallen into a support role over time. It was comfortable, even safe.

Now, though, thinking of how the music program was slipping away, of how one more thing she'd treasured and valued would no longer be a central role in her life, she wondered if she'd gotten too comfortable.

A heavy pause landed between them at the mention of the school's production. Fortunately, Jackson Bradford was tending bar tonight and had a way of making easy conversation with everyone who came into the restaurant.

"You guys eating here tonight or just having drinks?"

Or not. Jenna's heart began to race at the awkwardness of this simple question, but this time it was Travis who gave a casual shrug and said, "I wouldn't mind trying the menu." He jutted his chin toward the corner table where his grandmother was laughing at something Mr. Pritchard had said. "Besides, I don't think those two are going to be ready to leave for a while."

A date it was then. Or at least, dinner. Either way, she was happy it was happening.

"Was that you playing the piano earlier?" Jackson asked as Travis considered the food options. Jenna already knew the menu by heart, having eaten here hundreds of times over the years. The Bradfords were practically family, and they would be soon, when Britt and Jackson's younger brother Robbie tied the knot in the spring.

"I didn't realize it could be heard in here," Jenna said, feeling a little alarmed when she took in the full dining room.

"You kidding me? It's not often we get live music. I turned off the stereo so we could all enjoy it." Jackson gave her one of those grins that Jenna knew tended to work magic on most female tourists (and some locals) and turned his attention to Travis. "What'll it be?"

When their orders were placed, Travis turned his attention back to her. "Why don't you like to play in public?"

He wasn't going to let this go, but then, she supposed that she'd given him reason to ask, hadn't she?

"I'm a teacher now," she said. "It's not about my music, it's about what I can give to others."

"I'd say you gave quite a lot to the crowd back there." Travis grinned. "I don't think I've seen my grandmother smile for that length of time since...well, probably never. Probably not since my grandfather was still alive."

Jenna blinked at him, wondering if he was just saying that and realizing that he wasn't. That she had managed to bring joy to a lonely woman, not just to herself.

She glanced over her shoulder, where Mabel was once again laughing loudly. "I don't know. She seems to be pretty happy right now."

Travis raised his eyebrows. "I guess you're never too old for a second chance."

"Or to find love," Jenna said, and then stiffened, wishing she hadn't made that sudden change in the conversation.

He hesitated for a moment and then reached for his beer. "So, why is it that you don't play in public, aside from the events we already talked about?"

She swallowed hard and moved her napkin around on the wood surface of the bar. "I…I had a bad experience one time." When it was clear that he was waiting for her to elaborate, she took a breath. "When I was younger, I tried out for a music college. There was an audition, and…I froze. I panicked. I forgot the notes and I didn't have the sheet music, and…well, needless to say, I wasn't accepted."

He gave her a consolatory grin. "That must have been hard."

She nodded. "It was." Hard enough to make her not play the piano again for six months, for her to feel shaky and sweaty every time she sat down at the bench and held her fingers over the once familiar keys for a month after that. Hard enough to make her stay in this town, and eventually find a purpose in teaching others, hoping that for some of them, their fate would be better than hers.

"I guess you could say that was the point when I gave up my dreams."

He nodded slowly and picked up his beer. "Or maybe just reshaped them."

She sipped her cider, considering this. "I never thought of staying in my hometown as a different sort of dream, but I've made the most of it, and…I'm happy."

He peered at her. "Are you?"

No one had ever asked her this before, and it had been so long since she'd given up the aspiration to perform in concerts in big cities, or in the orchestra pit, that most of her friends and family had stopped mentioning it. At first, because it was such a sore subject, but later, because she'd never complained or brought up what might have been.

"It wasn't meant to be," she said.

"Oh now, I think anything is possible if we set our mind to it. Look at what this town is doing for the library," Travis pointed out. "When you want something enough, you find a way. It doesn't mean that it will turn out exactly as you hoped, but sometimes the new version is even better."

Jenna let those words soak in for a bit, thinking of how it might relate to her children's choir. Three songs weren't much, but if they were really special… Then there might be hope yet.

10

The Conway Orchard and Winery covered many acres of land on the edge of town, but the red barn at its center was its defining feature. It was here that Gabby had chosen to host this year's wreath-making event, on a quiet, snowy Monday night, when most people would be free of other plans.

Britt and Robbie had joined forces, offering cider and mulled wine to the crafters. Britt stopped Jenna as soon as she neared the table, still tired from her after-school lessons. Try as she might, not every child loved piano, and one of the young boys she taught on Mondays was more interested in playing soccer than practicing a musical instrument, despite his mother's insistence.

"Keira enjoyed last week's choir rehearsal," Britt said. "You must be disappointed about the pageant, though."

Jenna pulled in a breath. Somehow, she'd gotten through the day without thinking too much about what she had lost. Working on the Winter Carnival plans had helped—the old-fashioned theme was fun to think about, and with a bit of research, she'd compiled a list of games that were fitting with the Victorian period. So far all of the vendors she'd contacted had agreed to alter their menu slightly, or even just their presentation, to go along with the theme. It didn't hurt that she was related to so many of them, Britt included.

"I had you on my list to call today, but I ran out of time," Jenna said, dodging the sensitive topic. "Our theme for this year's carnival is a throwback, if you will, a Dickens-style Christmas."

"That's a brilliant idea!" Britt grinned. "It will certainly bring in the tourists."

"That, and hopefully remind people that what draws people to this town is the old-fashioned charm, the library included. It wouldn't be the same if we went and changed it all." She leaned in to whisper, "Believe it or not, it was Candy's idea."

"No!" Britt laughed. Of all her sisters, Britt had taken the longest to warm up to their father's girlfriend at first, but by the time Candy marched down the aisle and said "I do," she was possibly Candy's biggest fan. "People have a way of surprising you, don't they?"

You could say that again. Jenna glanced around the room, hoping that she was subtle in her search for Travis or his grandmother, only partially relieved when she didn't see either of them. Really, it would be for the best if they didn't show up—some distance would help her keep a clear head, focus on her new holiday mission, remember that her priority, as always, was with her music.

But was her heart?

She didn't have to consider that question for long because the barn doors opened, and, along with a cold gust of wind, came Travis and his grandmother.

"Who's that with Mabel Gibney?" Britt asked.

Jenna was grateful for an excuse to turn back to her cousin. "Oh, that's her grandson. And the temporary principal at the school."

"Oh, yes! I remember now. I saw him at the tree lighting." Britt nodded her understanding. "Keira speaks very highly of him. He's very popular with the kids."

Jenna wasn't sure why this surprised her, other than the part of her that still harbored her original opinion of him. The man she'd grown to know over the past week was quite different, though: warm, friendly, even a little thoughtful.

But still a Scrooge. Yes, still a Scrooge, even as he positioned his grandmother at the head of a craft table and set to work gathering greenery and pinecones for a holiday wreath.

"Well, I should go say hello to my sister and let you get back to it. I wanted to be sure to get some cider before it's gone." Before Jenna could forget, she dropped some cash in the donation jar. "All for a good cause!"

"But what about your good cause?" Britt poured handed her a mug.

Jenna swallowed back the emotions that threatened to show in her face and spoil her otherwise good spirits. "I have the Christmas choir, and the children are a part of it this year. But Christmas only comes once a year and I'm worried about what this means. What will happen next year if the kids don't have a music program at the school?"

Britt raised her eyebrows. "Let's hope it doesn't come to that, but if it does, then more of them will hopefully start taking piano lessons with you!"

Jenna wished it could be so simple, or that she could offer them all the wisdom and passion that Mr. Pritchard had installed in her to the students who did come to her, but not every child had that opportunity, and music was meant to be shared.

"Well, for now, let's focus on saving the library. Is that Helena?" Jenna spotted the librarian at one of the more crowded tables and waved, but Helena was too focused on tying a ribbon to look up and notice.

"You can be sure that her presence will keep Candy away tonight," Britt said knowingly. "Amelia has stopped paying Candy's late fines, and you know what a stickler Helena is about returning books. The last time I was at my dad's house, I saw at least three romance novels in the living room, and some of them were due back in October!"

Jenna laughed, but she didn't admit that she was relieved Candy wouldn't be present tonight. She didn't need anyone trying to insinuate that she and Travis would be a good match.

She looked at him across the room as he stood to gather more supplies. His thick brown hair was a complement to his camel-colored sweater that revealed broad shoulders and a washboard stomach, but it was the smile he gave her when he caught her eye that made her almost drop her beverage.

She held the copper mug a little tighter. Really, this was getting ridiculous. About as ridiculous as the fact that she'd put on her best jeans, dressy boots despite the six inches of snow that was expected to fall tonight, and a blouse that

Brooke had passed down to her from her New York days, making it the fanciest item of clothing in Jenna's closet.

"You seem to be making a habit of frequenting my family's places of business," she said as she approached the supply table, which was set out of earshot from the tables where people were busy talking and assembling, bow-tying, and hot-gluing.

"You're pretty hard to avoid," Travis said with a slow smile. "Not that I'm avoiding you."

She licked her bottom lip, realizing from the cock of his eyebrow that he was waiting for her response. "Are you implying that I'm avoiding you? Between the small size of this town and the abundance of community spirit, I probably couldn't do that even if I wished!"

"And is that what you wish? To avoid me?"

His eyes flickered with amusement as they held her gaze and a ripple of excitement tore through her stomach. He was flirting with her.

"Oh, I can't tell you that. Only Santa hears my Christmas wish." Her cheeks flamed as his mouth quirked with interest, and Jenna rushed to say, "It's hot in here, isn't it?"

It was indeed warm in the barn, which had been converted to a proper storefront years back for their Sunday market, fully equipped with heat, central air, and plumbing.

"We could step outside for a bit?" Travis suggested, surprising her. "The moon's bright enough that I might be able to see a bit of the property."

"Trying to take a break from the festivities?" she chided.

His grin was rueful. "That obvious?"

Jenna could never resist an opportunity to show off the land that had been in her family for generations. "All right then, but only because the smell of pine *is* a bit strong."

She was still wearing her coat, and Travis quickly found his on the hook near the door. Outside, the moon was bright, just as Travis had said it would be, and the snow fell gently, the flakes large enough to rest in her palm.

Jenna caught one, admiring the lacey details until it melted. "I love winter."

"It doesn't wear on you after a while?" he remarked. "I have to admit, Florida weather has been pretty nice."

She tried to keep her tone neutral when she said, "Think you'll go back soon then?"

"Florida?" He shook his head. "Nah. No reason for me to go back."

But did that mean he had a reason to stay here?

"Don't get me wrong. I love spring and summer, too. And fall." Jenna laughed. "Hey, I grew up on this orchard. Over there—" She pointed to the orchards that were dark now, impossible to see, even though Travis leaned in, trying to follow her direction. He was so close that she could feel the heat of his skin against the cold wind, and she didn't pull back, didn't want to.

"Rows and rows of apple trees," she said. "And back behind that other barn is the vineyard. My sisters and cousins and I used to play hide and seek for hours. And there—" Even though the cherry trees were on the other side of the barn where they stood, she wasn't ready to pull back just yet, instead saying, "Behind us are the cherry trees. We have something for every season."

"But not winter." He tipped his head. "So why would it be your favorite? And don't even think about saying Christmas," he added, flashing her a smile that made her stomach roll over a little.

She shrugged and took a sip of her warm beverage. "I'm a homebody, you could say. Winter is a good excuse to stay inside."

Her cousins and sisters would be sure to reprimand her if they heard her admitting this, but really, what was so wrong with loving to be home?

"Is that why you never auditioned again?" He tipped his head. "That story you told me last night, about the music college. Have you ever thought about giving it another try?"

Jenna swallowed hard. Staying in Blue Harbor hadn't been by choice, but somehow it had turned out for the better. "No, I never did. At first, I guess it was because of the rejection. If I'm being honest, maybe there's still a part of me that fears that."

"Doesn't everyone?"

She stared up at him, realizing that he had his own disappointments and maybe even insecurities, things in life that he had let hold him back, or maybe, kept him from moving forward. Because just moving wasn't the same at all, was it?

"I meant what I said about being happy here. Blue Harbor is my home. My family is all here, and it's nice to be around people who love and support you, no matter what." She pulled in a breath and stared up at the sky. "I don't think I could find that anywhere else."

"I can't imagine having an anchor like this," Travis said, his voice a little sad when he looked around at the many buildings and snow-covered fields.

"You have your grandmother's house," Jenna pointed out, but she knew it wasn't the same and that she was lucky, having ties to such a landmark in this community, something that was passed down through the generations, traditions that were honored.

She realized that Travis hadn't been given those opportunities and maybe this was why he didn't cherish things like she did.

"I didn't visit my grandmother much," he explained. "She and my mom, well, they had a tense relationship. I think my grandmother wanted her to stay in town, and my mom wanted to get out, explore."

"Your mom sounded adventurous," Jenna said, smiling.

A strange look passed over Travis's eyes. "I think she was restless. Maybe even unhappy. She didn't want to be tied down, not to a small town, but sometimes not even to a big city. But it was more than that. She couldn't stick with a job or a relationship." He frowned, looking down at the ground.

Jenna set a hand on his elbow, leaving it there. "She stuck with you."

His smile was sad when he looked up at her. "Yeah. She did. And she loved her mother. She just couldn't stay here. This town wasn't enough for her, even though it's everything to my grandmother."

"Your grandmother has lost a lot, but the people of this town have kept her smiling." Jenna thought about that for a moment. In many ways, the same could be said for herself.

"She has a good community here," Travis agreed. Then, with a little grin, he said, "And I'm beginning to think that she might be finding more than just a friend in Mr. Pritchard."

Jenna laughed. "You think? It's sweet, isn't it? There's no better time to fall in love than at Christmastime."

Immediately, Jenna was grateful for the darkness that hopefully made it impossible for Travis to see the blush rise up in her cheeks. He looked at her strangely, his gaze lingering for long enough to cause her breath to slow and her heart to speed up.

"Is that so?" he said, his mouth twitching.

"Well, sure, I mean…" *Oh, brother.* "Christmas is the time for magic, as they say."

"That it is," he said, nodding.

A car door slammed and Jenna looked over to see her sister Gabby approaching, carrying an oversized boxed filled with greenery.

"Gabby?" She glanced at Travis and explained. "My sister."

"Ah yes, from the tree lighting." He nodded, and she could have sworn his eyes twinkled in the moonlight.

The heat in Jenna's face notched higher and she stepped toward her sister. "You need help?"

Gabby craned her neck around the box. "You came!" she exclaimed, then, doing a double-take at Travis, she said bluntly. "You!"

Oh, dear.

Travis grinned, game for whatever came next. Jenna, however, was inwardly cringing. Now that Gabby was happily settled into a relationship of her own, any eligible man was by default someone she thought Jenna should get to know.

Travis held open the door and the women filed into the barn. Jenna half wished Travis wouldn't join them, but there he was, right behind her.

"I didn't realize that you two were here *together*," Gabby's eyes widened on Jenna as she set the box down on the supply table and dusted her hands off on her coat.

"We're on the planning committee so it makes sense to attend these events and help where needed," Jenna said at the same time that Travis said, "I'm here with my grandmother."

Jenna glanced at him, sharing a little smile. So they were both on the spot. Something in common then.

"Well, I should probably make sure that everyone has enough supplies, but Travis, we could use a strong guy like you to help carry the boxes of the finished wreaths out to the loading dock. I'm going to stop by tomorrow to collect everything. I have a feeling that I'll be too tired tonight by the time we're finished."

"At your service." Travis nodded.

"I'll see you Wednesday night?" Gabby asked Jenna.

The cookie swap! It had almost slipped her mind. Thinking quickly of all the commitments she already had for the week, Jenna nodded. "Wouldn't miss it! It's only one of the best nights of the year!"

"What's Wednesday night?" Travis asked once Gabby had walked away, looking back only twice to give Jenna less than subtle expressions.

"The cookie swap party I'd told you about." Jenna started sorting pine sprigs from boxwood. "I guess that means I'll have to find some time to bake cookies between now and then."

"You don't want to just pick up a box at the store?"

Jenna laughed. "I can't do that!"

"Why not?" Travis shrugged. "If they taste good, what would it matter?"

"It would matter because baking cookies is something you do this time of year. It's fun and festive and, well, everyone associates Christmas with cookies!" She shook her head, sensing that she'd lost him. "Oh, but that's right. You're not into all the fun activities that make Christmas so special."

"I happen to have nothing against cookies," he said.

"Oh, no. My cookies are for the party. Besides, I can't take any cookies from the swap unless I bring some. Those are the rules."

"What if I offered up some cookies of my own? Would you let me have a taste then?"

Now he had her full attention. "You mean to tell me that you're willing to tie on an apron and roll out some dough just to get a few samples of what I take home from the party?"

"I'd rather try the ones you make, but...yes." He grinned. "If you'll let me be a part of your tradition, that is."

She was hesitant to show just how willing she would be to alter her plans. "I only have tomorrow night to bake them—"

"I'm free any time after four." He grinned broadly as if knowing he'd gotten his way.

She glanced at him, wondering how she could even say no and if she wanted to. "Your grandmother would probably like some Christmas cookies, considering that she did happen to win a beautiful platter from Harbor Holidays last year in the carnival raffle."

"So I guess we're making cookies?" Travis looked at her for agreement, and she didn't see how or why she should resist.

"I guess we are," she said, hiding her smile behind a big box that she then carried over to Helena's table, where services other than flirting were required.

Jenna arrived at Mabel Gibney's house with two grocery bags of ingredients, a recipe torn from a magazine she'd found at her parents' house, and a thumping heart. In past years, she'd baked cookies in between her after-school lessons, always setting aside an extra dozen for the children she taught as an incentive for working hard. She wasn't used to sharing the activity with anyone else, especially not a man, and especially not an attractive one.

She walked along the cleared brick path, which, judging from the snow that continued to fall, had been freshly shoveled. It warmed her heart to think this gesture may have been made on account of her arrival.

Or maybe Travis had just decided to take on the task when he arrived home from the school.

The answer was obvious when he opened the door before she even had a chance to ring the bell. The smile on his face told her what she'd already suspected, and made her take a deep breath of crisp winter air to settle herself. They were just baking cookies, even if that had started to feel like code for another excuse to spend time together.

"I brought supplies," she said, lifting the bags, which he promptly took from her.

"Great!" He set them down in the front hall and closed the door behind her as she took off her coat. "I stopped by the store as well but I'm not sure if I bought anything useful."

She handed him her coat, which he hooked onto the coat rack. He was looking at her funny, his arm still raised, and for a moment she wondered what he was doing, if he was trying to reach out to her, hug her or something in greeting—had they reached that point?

Instead, he brushed softly at her hair. "You've got some snow…"

"Oh." Of course. He wasn't going to hug her! That would be, well, weird, right? She patted her head hastily, feeling the snowflakes melt under her touch.

To think she'd spent time on her hair before coming here today. When all they were doing was baking cookies…

"Is your grandmother here?" She glanced around the hallway and into the rooms that flanked it.

"She's next door," he explained. He lifted an eyebrow. "She felt very strongly about it. Invited herself over, if I'm not mistaken."

Jenna fought back a smile. Was everyone in this town a matchmaker? But then, no doubt Travis's grandmother was hoping that if he met someone special, he'd stay on past Suzanne's return.

If Suzanne returned. Hadn't that been implied?

She jutted her head to the tree in the living room that nearly filled the bay window. "I'm happy to see you do indeed have a tree and a beautiful one at that," she remarked.

"I was a little worried that I'd swiped the last good one out from under you."

"Oh, if I had to drive to the nearest forest and cut one down myself, my grandmother was going to have a nice tree."

"Did you help her decorate it, too?"

"I'll have you know that I carried all the boxes down from the attic, unpacked them, helped decorate, and there might have even been some Christmas music on in the background. Her idea," he added. He gestured for her to follow him to the back of the house.

Jenna stayed back for a moment to admire the tree from the short distance. The lights were a little unevenly spread, and the ornaments were mostly clustered near the bottom of the tree, leading her to assume that Travis had been in charge of the lights while Mabel handled the rest.

"Still don't see the point in it, though," Travis said as he walked down the hall. "That thing will be dried up and dead by the end of next week."

"And by then Christmas will be over," Jenna said, realizing that not only would the holiday and all its anticipation be over, but possibly this time she was spending with Travis too. "Besides, the fun of having a tree is decorating it."

"Oh, you call it fun, do you?" He turned and looked at her frankly. "I was standing on a ladder for close to forty-five minutes trying to get that star topper just right while Gran ordered me around from the comfort of the sofa."

Jenna laughed. "Did you finally meet her approval?"

"Barely. She's a tough one to please." He shook his head, but she could see that he was smiling.

"Your dedication to your grandmother is admirable," she said as she took one last look at the tree, complete with a topper and strings of lights she could now picture him untangling while Mabel looked on impatiently.

She nearly laughed at the image, but when she reached the doorway to the kitchen, she stopped in her place. There, spread out on the island, was every kind of sugar, flour, oil, and spice that the local market shelved.

"Wow," she said when she found her voice. Her gaze rested on a few of the spice containers as she neared: turmeric, cumin, paprika. She slapped a hand to her mouth.

"What is it? These won't work?" He stopped unpacking her bags and looked at her in alarm.

"Oh, they'll work all right, if you're cooking a spicy dinner." She shook her head. He hadn't been stretching the truth when he'd said he'd never baked before.

"Oh." His cheeks went a little pink but he laughed, too.

"Here." She gently moved toward him, aware that in the tight space in the corner of the kitchen, between the island and the sink, they were close, very close, close enough for her to smell the soap on his skin from his morning shower, the wool from his sweater, and sense the warmth from his body.

Forget needing that paprika to heat up a cold winter afternoon.

She reached for some of the spices she'd brought. "Cinnamon, nutmeg, cloves. These are the flavors of Christmas."

"The flavors of Christmas," he laughed. "Sounds like the name of a cookbook. Oh!"

Before she was ready for him to break this physical proximity, he moved across the room to a baker's rack and held up a weathered and frayed recipe book.

"Right before you came over, I was looking through these books for a recipe and I found this. It was my grandmother's."

"May I?" Intrigued, Jenna stepped forward, taking the book from his hand. She opened it carefully, in case the pages were loose, which they were. Random slips of paper, newspaper clippings dating back forty or more years, and index cards that bore stains were tucked inside the book, which had evidently been much used and well loved. "Does she still use this?"

Travis shook his head. "Not since I've been here. Most nights, she just fixes some toast and tea. I feel bad that I'm not much of a cook." His expression bore his regret. "I offer to take her out, but she prefers the comforts of home, as she likes to say."

"Don't we all?"

Travis shrugged, showing he wasn't so convinced. "Since we moved around so much when I was a kid, I never really had a home base to fall back on once I was an adult and out of the house. My apartments aren't exactly filled with throw pillows or—"

"Christmas trees?" she wagered a guess.

His smile was wry. "That noticeable?"

"Just a little." She tipped her head. "You mentioned that you didn't plan to go back to Florida, but you can't think of one place that stood out, one that you could call home?"

"I guess I haven't found it yet. But being here, I'm starting to understand why my grandmother has preferred to stay. There's something to be said for having a house full of memories and photos. My grandfather's been gone for decades but sometimes something in this house still sparks something in Gran, and it's like, she comes alive. Like he's still with her when she sees or hears something that reminds her of him. They had a lot of happy memories in this house."

Jenna closed the book and held it to her chest. "All the more reason to surprise her with her favorite Christmas cookie. I'm sure there's one in here that holds special meaning, or will remind her of a happy time, one that doesn't have to be forgotten."

She could tell from the way this afternoon was going that the recipe she was planning to try would forever be marked by this occasion, and that long after Travis had gone off to wherever life took him, she would bake these cookies and remember the Christmas that she spent with Scrooge himself.

Even if she was starting to suspect he had a little spirit tucked away in him after all.

*

When the cookies were in the oven and the timer was set, Travis wondered if it would be too much to offer Jenna a glass of wine and decided that he should, and not just because her family owned a winery.

Yes, wine sometimes implied a date, but he'd be lying to himself if this wasn't starting to feel like one—and possibly the best one he'd ever had. He didn't invest much in them usually, knowing that there was little chance of things developing into a relationship, little desire to form that kind of a bond that would only have to be broken next time he moved. His ex had been a lot like him, making it easy to fall into a daily routine, until she'd started asking for more than he could give.

"Just one glass," she demurred when he uncorked the bottle. "I'm driving, though I could have walked, seeing how close your grandmother's house is from town."

"Is this your first time over here?" He filled two glasses partway and handed her one.

She took a sip, nodding. "Unless you count caroling."

His eyes shot up to her. "Caroling? Oh, I seem to recall my grandmother mentioning this, but I didn't put it all together."

"The Christmas choir carols every Christmas Eve. It's—"

"Tradition," he finished, matching her grin. "Well, my grandmother looks forward to it. She's already talking about."

"This year will be extra special, with the costumes. And Candy suggested caroling around the carnival, which you might have seen in one of her many emails."

"Ah, yes, the costumes. I might have to go up to the attic and rummage around for more than decorations."

"I think you'd look rather handsome in a topcoat and hat." Jenna's cheeks flushed as she took another sip of wine. "I should check on the cookies…"

She turned on the oven light and peered inside, giving him a chance to let his gaze linger on her figure, her hair, for one moment before she turned and flashed him that radiant smile.

"Only a few more minutes. We need to watch them so they don't burn. We wouldn't want to have to start over."

"I'm in no rush." If burnt cookies meant another half hour with Jenna, he'd take it. She was easy to talk to, kind, and though he'd never admit it, her passion for the holidays was starting to rub off on him, unlike his last girlfriend, who was as apathetic to all the fanfare as he was. Or had been.

Still, there was the unspoken tension, and music was as much a part of her life as his career was to him.

"How is the children's choir coming along?" he asked carefully.

She looked at him in surprise but then nodded enthusiastically. "Wonderful! I mean, we've only had one rehearsal, but we made it count, and this week I'll meet with everyone Thursday and Friday night, so we get a final run-through the night before the carnival kicks off. I'm making it a special tribute to Mr. Pritchard. He inspired me so much, that it feels right to honor him this way before his retirement at the end of the school year."

"That will mean a lot to him. And I promise I won't mention it to my grandmother. I think those two have been canoodling on the phone."

"Canoodling?" Jenna laughed, and Travis couldn't help but smile. "It is a surprise of sorts, so thanks for not saying anything. We're doing three of Mr. Pritchard's favorite carols. The children have sung them before, so they won't need much practice. I'm just hoping I can wrap up everything before the bonfire."

"The bonfire?" He looked at her with interest.

"Over at the yacht club. They have this beautiful lawn, looking out over the lake with a view of Evening Island. Every season they have food and drinks and fire pits set up for guests. This Friday they're donating all the proceeds to the library fund."

"It's amazing how the community pulled together like this, and so quickly."

Travis was surprised, but Jenna wasn't. "That's Blue Harbor for you. There's no other place like it."

"You think they'll get a good turnout?"

"It's on the eve of the Winter Carnival, so I'm sure of it."

"Well, I am on the planning committee," he said, the corner of his mouth tipping into a grin.

She nodded sagely. "It is our duty to attend these events and make sure everything is running smoothly."

"Our duty, absolutely."

Their eyes locked for a moment and he took a step forward, but the sound of the oven timer startled them both, and Jenna quickly grabbed an oven mitt.

"Just in time!" she said triumphantly, setting the cookie sheet on the stovetop to cool before going back for another one.

Just in time, he thought, only he wasn't thinking of the cookies. He was thinking of the fact that he'd almost kissed her, wanted to kiss her, and that if he had that would just make everything much more complicated than it needed to be.

*

The next night, with a plastic container filled with cookies heavy in her arms, Jenna met Brooke downstairs in the bridal shop so they could walk down Main Street together. Amelia's house was near the center of town, and it was always the gathering place for the annual cookie party. Mostly, this was because Amelia liked to host the event, but it was also tradition by now, and when they could, Jenna and her cousins liked to uphold traditions, even when they introduced some new ones along the way.

"Are we stopping to meet Gabby along the way?" Jenna asked as Brooke locked up the shop. She paused to admire the glistening wedding gown in the window, that sparkled like the snow on the branches in the moonlight.

Catching Brooke's eye, she quickly looked away. She was getting ahead of herself. Travis was a friend. And likely a temporary one at that.

"She had to run a delivery out to Pine Falls," Brooke told her. "She'll be a little late to the party, which means she might be stuck with my store-bought sugar cookies."

"You didn't!"

Brooke grimaced and held up her container. "I did. But it was just the dough. I rolled them out myself and…"

"And?" Jenna raised an eyebrow. Unless she'd completely transformed the dough, Amelia would be onto her with just one bite.

"And sprinkled them with sugar?"

Jenna laughed. "I suppose I can't fault you. Last year I did pretty much the same, only I might have frosted them."

"As much as I love the idea of baking Christmas cookies, I haven't found the time with the new business and all the local festivities. Speaking of which, how's the carnival planning coming along? That principal still bothering you, because if he is—"

"Oh." Jenna looked straight ahead, knowing that if she met her sister's eye, Brooke would see straight through to her innermost thoughts. "He's not so bad."

"Well, considering that I hear he's Mabel's grandson, I doubt she'd let him get away with anything," Brooke chuckled. "Shame, though. He's cute, don't you think?"

Jenna was grateful to see they were already almost at their destination. She wasn't sure she could feign nonchalance much longer, especially when she agreed wholeheartedly: Travis was very handsome indeed.

"Looks like we're the late arrivals!" She nudged her chin toward Amelia's front window, which was framed in lights, glowing from inside where several of their cousins were already visible, laughing and holding wine glasses.

"Dodging my question, are you?" Brooke said pertly as they climbed the stairs.

"What?" Jenna frowned. "No. I mean, what's there to say? Travis is here while Suzanne tends to family matters.

Once she's back, he'll be gone. Does it matter if he's handsome or not?"

"Does it?" Brooke fought back a smile. "And I think the word I used was cute."

Jenna pinched her lips and reached for the door handle, knowing that they were expected and there was no need to knock. Amelia turned from the adjacent living room and hurried toward the door, lifting the containers from their hands and setting them on the buffet table she'd set up against the wall while they hung their coats on the hook in the small entryway.

"These are pretty! I don't think I've ever seen them before." Amelia bent forward to smell the freshly baked cookies.

"Those are pretty!" Natalie Clark was next through the door, with her sister Bella.

"Almost too pretty to eat," Bella remarked.

"They're an old recipe," Jenna said vaguely to Maddie, who was equally curious as she approached.

"I've seen these before!" Maddie insisted, looking from the cookies to Amelia to Jenna. "Years back, Mrs. Gibney used to make cookies and drop them off for some of her friends as gifts. I can remember my grandmother giving me one when I was over her house."

Must have been their grandmother on their mother's side, because Jenna, unfortunately, had no such memories.

"Oh, you're right! I can't believe I forgot about them. They were so buttery, I didn't dare chew." Amelia glanced at Jenna. "May I?"

"Of course!" Jenna flushed at the attention because no one had ever paid much attention to her contribution at the cookie swap before. Still, now that she'd been appropriately flattered, she hoped these memories didn't stir up further questions about the origin of the recipe.

"Wherever did you find the recipe?" Maddie asked, and then, her face teased into a smile when she realized she already knew the answer. "Mrs. Gibney is Travis's grandmother, isn't she?"

Jenna pinched her lips. Like the rest of the town by this point, Maddie knew good and well that Mabel was his grandmother. "We thought we'd bake them for her since they were one of her favorite Christmas cookies."

"We?" Maddie blinked, feigning innocence.

"Travis doesn't know how to bake, and I had to make cookies anyway, and—" And she was making too many excuses for an innocent few hours. Or maybe not completely innocent, she thought, pulling up an image of that moment in the kitchen when she thought something might have happened between them. "We baked the cookies together if that answers your question."

"Oh, but it's just sparked many more!" Maddie grinned as she popped a peanut butter cookie into her mouth and chewed.

Amelia, always one to let people talk when they were good and ready, just set a hand on Jenna's shoulder and walked over to tend to the fire.

"What are we talking about?" Gabby, still in her coat with the chill on its soft cashmere fabric, set some cut-out cookies on the table.

"Your sister's new love life," Maddie said casually.

"What's this?" Gabby reached for a brownie, as Jenna knew she would, and took a large bite, chewing slowly while she waited for Jenna to speak.

"It's nothing. I spent a little time with Travis Dunne and suddenly everyone's planning my wedding."

"What's this about a wedding?" Brooke leaned over the table, clearly interested in more than the cookie selection.

Noticing this, Maddie shook her head, walked into the kitchen, and returned with another platter of them. "Good thing I made another batch. No matter how many new recipes I experiment with, everyone just wants these candy cane brownies!"

"You've started a new tradition," Jenna said, happy for her, and hoping that the topic had safely been dropped.

"And maybe you are, too," Maddie seemed to have an internal battle with herself before finally picking up a brownie for herself. "You'd think I'd be sick of these things, but I'm not."

"So, you've been spending time with Travis. And here I thought you had just decided not to completely hate him." Brooke looked at her suspiciously.

"Baking cookies is a rather festive thing to do," Gabby said coyly. "I take it that he's not a Scrooge after all?"

Jenna sighed, but she couldn't completely hide her smile. She had enjoyed her time with Travis, baking, laughing, enjoying the ease of his company. Just like she'd enjoyed every other interaction she'd had with him these past couple of weeks, not that she'd been sharing details with this group.

Unfortunately for her, she didn't have to.

"Oh, Travis was the one from the bookshop!" Bella grinned. "Very handsome."

Jenna didn't think that Maddie could physically lift her eyebrows higher if she tried. "So you went shopping together?"

"And out to dinner!" Candy cried out, giving Jenna a playful bump of her hip to scoot her away.

"Candy!" Amelia looked understandably stunned. This was a holiday tradition, typically reserved for ten cousins and some of their friends. Candy was technically of the next generation, even though her age was hazy and she refused to admit it to anyone.

"Oh, you don't mind, do you, Amelia?" Candy bit down on a knuckle, clearly feeling no remorse in the least. She wasted no time in shedding her coat. "I've had this idea for a recipe for the café and I thought, wouldn't the cookie swap be the perfect excuse to give it a whirl?"

Amelia glanced at Britt, who just hooded her eyes and took a deep sip of her wine. "Of course, Candy." She smiled graciously. "What do you have for us tonight?"

"I'll get to that in a moment. First, I want to hear all about Jenna's new man!"

Jenna stifled an eye roll and picked up a plate. "If this is how the evening is going, then I'm going to need some sugar, first."

"And a cocktail." Gabby grinned and picked up a martini glass filled with something that smelled like eggnog but was clearly enhanced.

Soon, they were all gathered near the crackling fire, all sets of eyes in the room latched onto Jenna. And here she'd hoped the library would be the topic of discussion tonight.

"First impressions aren't always what they seem," Candy said wisely. "When I met Denny—" Here, Jenna's cousins exchanged a glance, because to everyone else, he was just Dennis.

"When I first met Denny, I had to be so strict with that man! Why, he had just broken his limbs, was supposed to be in bed, and he kept trying to chase me around that kitchen!"

Another glance from the cousins. Jenna hid her smile by taking another sip of wine.

"I had to wave that wooden spoon at him and tell him that if he didn't follow Nurse Candy's orders, there would be no special surprises. And I'm so good at surprises." She giggled.

"I didn't realize you were a nurse, Candy," Heidi said, frowning in confusion.

Britt slid her eyes to the youngest of the Clarks. "Caregiver."

"Anyway," Candy continued. "I'm sure that man thought I was no fun at all. And we all know how much fun I am."

The girls all murmured their agreement. Candy was many things, and fun was definitely one of them.

"Sometimes first impressions are wrong," Heidi pointed out, and in this case, Jenna suspected that she was referring to her colorful work history that sometimes made

for awkward interview questions. "And it isn't his fault that the school's struggling to fund the music program."

Natalie gave a little smile. "He's pretty handsome. If you aren't interested…"

Jenna's pulse flicked with something strangely close to jealousy, and before she had time to think of a casual comment, Britt cut in: "Natalie! He's your daughter's school principal. Don't you think that would be a conflict of interest?"

"Love is complicated." Natalie shrugged. "Besides, he's only the temporary principal."

Jenna stayed quiet as she sipped her drink. Natalie was right, he was only holding the position temporarily, but she was also right about something else.

Love—if that's what she was starting to feel for him—was indeed complicated.

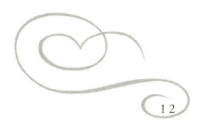

By Friday, the fact that it was the last choir rehearsal before the Winter Carnival wasn't lost on Jenna, and she decided to prioritize the children over the adults, who were much more capable of practicing on their own and who had nearly perfected every song in last night's rehearsal, making tonight's run smooth and easy.

This didn't stop Candy from tapping Jenna on the shoulder and asking if they could have one more run-through of "Deck the Halls."

"I didn't hit that final note just right," Candy explained.

Jenna refrained from pointing out that Candy hadn't exactly hit any of the notes just right, but instead she glanced at the clock and gave a nod. "We'll take it from the second verse."

She lifted her hands and, waiting until Candy had scooted back into position, started to play. Of course, the choir would be singing a capella when they went door to door, but while they were practicing, she preferred to lead them through each song. She also preferred to play than to sing, but she joined in anyway, even though her voice, like so many others in the group, was drowned out by Candy's never-shy vocals.

Jenna glanced up as they hit the last few bars, Candy's passion swayed her far to the left side, then, on the next note, far to the right. More than one of the other members inched out of her way, and Jenna had to stop singing for a moment in case she burst out laughing instead.

"Better?" Candy asked once Jenna pushed back from her piano stool.

"Much." Really, it hadn't been any different than the first time, with possibly the exception of Candy's enthusiasm. Jenna liked to believe that there was some level of musical talent in everyone, just waiting to be discovered. Candy, however, was testing that theory.

Still, everyone deserved to enjoy music, and Jenna had made that just as much a part of her teachings as she had technique. Mr. Pritchard had instilled that in her.

She wondered idly if she'd see Mr. Pritchard at the bonfire event tonight. Considering that Travis was going, she couldn't see him leaving his grandmother behind.

With a flutter in her chest, Jenna arranged her music sheets. The children had all arrived by now, and she was eager to run through this weekend's event with props, even if meant that she would have to stay a little later than she'd planned.

As they shuffled into their assigned places, some already forgetting where they should go, Jenna longed for the camaraderie she had shared over the years with Mr. Pritchard, who was always at her side, helping the children along, calling out the next song, or, on the night of the big event, stage whispering from behind the curtain.

Her heart was just turning heavy when Candy came speed-walking toward her. There was nothing Candy did halfheartedly.

Jenna opened her mouth to explain she needed to focus on the children now, but Candy just picked up a box of the battery-operated candles and said, "I'm happy to help the kids with these if you want."

"You don't need to get to the bonfire?"

Candy had only talked about it in between every song, how "Denny" would be waiting for her.

"It won't kill him to sit in the cold for a few extra minutes," Candy said lightly. She gave a coy grin. "Besides, he knows I'll be warming him up the moment I arrive, and I don't mean with a blanket."

Oh, brother. Still, Jenna couldn't deny the thought of sitting close to Travis was at the forefront of her mind.

Candy sashayed over to the children and began handing out the candles, instructing a few of the younger ones on how to turn it on and off, and reminding all of them to be quiet until Jenna was seated at her piano and ready to give them the signal. The signal they'd all come to learn was extended eye contact followed by a single nod.

Jenna smiled her gratitude and moved back to the piano, but Candy was quick on her heels.

"Will I be seeing you at the bonfire tonight?" Candy batted her lashes as she leaned onto the piano ledge.

Knowing that Candy wasn't going to back down without an answer, and knowing that within the next hour, Candy would have her answer, Jenna sighed and said, "I plan to stop by."

"And will anyone else we know be there?" Candy wanted to know.

Jenna straightened her music sheets, arranging them in order of the three songs, even though she had every note memorized by now. "Oh, of course. All the girls will be there," she said, referring to the Conways and Clarks.

Candy nodded. "I was wondering if any guys will be there. Single ones. Maybe a certain one that is related to our dear Mabel Gibney?"

"Most of Blue Harbor will be there," Jenna said with a smile. "I'm sure we're bound to run into Travis."

"I hope so," Candy said with a little smile.

Jenna positioned her hands over the keys and took a deep breath before glancing at the clock once more.

She certainly hoped so too.

*

Travis hadn't been surprised that his grandmother asked to go to the bonfire, and he was happy that it saved him from having to admit to her that he was already planning to go—that would only lead to a full inquisition. She hadn't been shy in saying that she hoped he would like it enough here to stay. And he hadn't been shy in telling her that wasn't even necessarily an option. There was a board meeting next Monday where he'd find out more about the school's plans, something that he hadn't paid much credence to, until recently.

He pulled in a breath as he parked the car and killed the engine. Staying in one place for too long usually meant disappointment, and getting close only led to heartache. But he'd meant what he'd said about there being something special about this town…and the people in it.

Travis pushed his door open against the arctic wind and hurried around the car to help his grandmother from the passenger side. He'd only started to unload the wheelchair from the trunk when she gave him one of her sharp looks.

"I don't see how you're going to get that thing over the lawn," she huffed.

"I was able to get it through the town square for the tree lighting festival," he pointed out. "I also seem to recall you balking at me when I worried the very same."

She gave him a rueful look and raised her chin. "All the same, I think I'll walk tonight."

Travis stared at her and then dropped his gaze to her feet, where sure enough, she'd worn snow boots rather than her usual loafers. Perhaps it had been in the plan all along. The question was why, and why now? The most she ever walked around the house was to stand up to lift the kettle from the stove for tea, and she'd long ago stopped using the upstairs bedrooms, turning the den into her personal space instead.

"I'm not sure that's such a good idea," he said tensely, looking at the salted pavement and then on to the paper lantern-lined path that had been cut away in the snow.

"The cold air gives me energy," she said, motioning for him to hand her the cane that he had assumed would be left in the car.

FINDING CHRISTMAS

Against his better judgment, Travis folded up the wheelchair, set it back in the trunk, and took his grandmother's elbow. "We'll go slowly," he said.

His grandmother wasn't paying him any attention by now. Her eyes were darting, and he had to admit, she moved at a brisker pace than he expected, as if she were eager to get to her destination.

It wasn't until she broke out into a smile that Travis looked up and realized the real reason behind her sudden declaration and good mood. Mr. Pritchard was pushing himself up from a bench, standing to greet her, his eyes so trained on his date for this evening that he didn't even seem to notice Travis until they were standing shoulder to shoulder.

"You look lovely," he said, taking her hand. He motioned to the bench that was positioned in front of a fire. "I thought this would be easier for us than those Adirondack chairs the youngsters sit in."

"I think if I were to sit in one of those, I'd never get up again!"

Travis startled at his grandmother's laughter, which seemed to float over the quiet snow, fading into the crackling and popping of the logs.

"I see I was just the chauffeur tonight," he teased her.

She settled herself onto the bench and covered her legs with the wool blanket Mr. Pritchard passed to her, before sliding beside her.

"It did you good to come here tonight," she said, that old spark back in her eye. "But yes, I'm afraid you'll have to find someone else to share it with. Someone special for a special night."

Travis knew he should correct her then and there, tell her that he had already found someone special, that it hadn't worked out, and that he was fine on his own. But he'd be lying, and he never misled his grandmother, and not just because she'd see right through it. She was the kindest woman he knew and seeing her like this, downright girlish and happy, he took it as his cue to back away.

"I'm meeting Jenna Conway if you must know," he said, sensing no surprise in her reaction. "But then, you might have guessed that."

"You two have been spending a lot of time together," Gran said.

"It's been nice to find a friend in Blue Harbor," Travis admitted.

"You won't find a better girl than our Jenna," Mr. Pritchard said. "She's a true talent, that one. Haven't met a pupil or parent who doesn't adore the work she does with the kids. Truth be told, I plan to nominate her for my position upon my retirement this spring. I couldn't think of a better candidate for the job. But, well."

Gran was shaking her head. "Such a shame to think that the board would even consider doing away with the music program."

"It is," Travis agreed.

"And is there really nothing that you can do?" She'd pressed him on this nearly as much as Jenna, especially now that she had a vested interest thanks to the man sitting beside her.

"My position is temporary," Travis replied. "And now I'll leave you two to enjoy the evening." He slipped away before any more could be said on the tense topic that somehow he and Jenna had managed to shelve, but probably not forget if he was being honest with himself.

He spotted her coming up the lit pathway, wearing a heavy down parka and earmuffs. Her long dark hair hung in waves at her shoulders, and for a moment, it was as if none of that conversation had just happened, as if none of those problems existed, and maybe, no one else existed.

*

Jenna joined Travis at the top of the path, noticing his grandmother watching with a strained neck in the near distance.

"Looks like Mr. Pritchard isn't having such a lonely Christmas after all," she said, pleased.

"That makes two of us." Travis slid her a grin and Jenna glanced away, her heart beating quickly.

"It's a nice clear night for this," Jenna said, suddenly feeling shy. She shivered as she lowered herself onto the Adirondack chair. "I'm daring to think we may just be able to save the library in the end."

"Really?" He looked surprised but pleased as he sat beside her, close enough that his arm brushed hers. "My grandmother used to take me to that library when I was little. Maybe that's why I developed such a fondness for books and eventually academia."

Jenna grinned at him, wanting to learn more about that boy who had visited, and how it had shaped him. "It's important for children to have an outlet."

He nodded. "Consistency. Not that I have any now. But books, music, it's something you can take with you anywhere. It's a way to escape, sure, but it's also a way to find your place."

She held his gaze, knowing that they were touching upon a sensitive topic, and one that she wasn't so sure she wanted to get into just now, not when it was such a lovely cold night and the fire was so warm.

A gust of wind blew in off the lake and she shivered again. For a moment, she wondered if Travis might put his arm around her, but instead, he jumped to his feet. "There are some blankets near the bar stand. Why don't I grab one for you?"

Jenna didn't protest. She warmed her hands over the crackling flames while she watched him walk away, toward the entrance, pausing to select a large wool blanket and then stopping again at the bar. He hadn't asked her order, but she didn't mind. Lately, she liked feeling surprised, and she knew that anything that the Yacht Club was serving was bound to be delicious.

He came back a few minutes later with two steaming mugs and the blanket tucked under his arm. She carefully took the mulled wine from him and then the blanket, stiffening only slightly as he helped it arrange it over her lap.

"You won't be cold?"

"Nah. I have this super warm coat." He patted the rather thin wool coat he wore and suppressed a shudder. "Between the hot drink and the fire, I'm set."

She resisted a smile. "I guess the winters don't get this cold down south."

"Nope." He laughed. "I thought I liked that, being able to slip into flip-flops on the weekends, not ever really worrying about grabbing a coat most days of the year, but being here, I'm reminded of how much I enjoy the change of seasons."

"I'm not so ready for this one to change just yet." Jenna sighed. All around them were other couples, families, gathered around the small fire pits, some roasting marshmallows, others watching the flames crackle and dance. Most of the trees of the property had been wrapped in twinkling lights, illuminating the nearby lake that caught the moonlight up above. Somewhere in the distance, she could make out a few lights on Evening Island, where she knew their snow-filled center of town also boasted a community tree, even if it wasn't quite as grand and celebrated as the one here in Blue Harbor. "Fall is beautiful, especially on the orchard, and spring is special, especially when all the lilacs and cherry trees bloom. But Christmas is…magical."

"I thought you didn't believe in magic."

She was surprised he remembered her saying that. Surprised by a lot of things. "I guess, I'm starting to change my mind…" She pulled in a breath as their eyes locked.

She caught herself, realized that she'd probably gone a little too far. Beside her, Travis was giving her a curious look, but at least he wasn't laughing at her romantic notions.

Instead, he said, "I thought Christmases like this only existed in movies. I guess you could say I never really understood all the hype until now."

She sat back to give him a proper look. "Why, Mr. Dunne, did you just admit that you have found your Christmas spirit?

He laughed, then shook his head. "I wouldn't go that far, but I guess that if Christmas means more nights like this, then, yes. It's something I've been looking forward to and…it's something I don't want to end." His gaze lingered on hers for a beat longer than casual.

"Me either," Jenna whispered, even though she wasn't so sure they were even talking about the holiday anymore or if they were talking about something else, something more personal.

He leaned in ever so slightly, enough to make her heart speed up. Their chairs were arm to arm, and they were close enough for her to see the curl of his eyelashes as his gaze dropped from her eyes to her mouth, before he reached over to adjust the blanket on their laps.

"There you are, Jenna!"

Startled, Jenna looked up to see Candy staring down at her, alarm in her big blue eyes. "Oh, I am so sorry to interrupt what appeared to be a very *close* moment!"

Jenna didn't dare to look at Travis, who had now pushed back against his chair, leaving a space where his body had just been.

"I waited, and I didn't want to have to intrude..." Candy continued.

Jenna blinked at her. "You were watching us?"

"Just over there behind that boxwood," Candy said. "I was waiting for a moment—"

And this had seemed like a good moment? Jenna closed her eyes and took one of the calming breaths that her sister Brooke had mastered while designing Candy's wedding gown last spring...about two dozen times.

"What is it, Candy?" She made a silent plea that it wasn't something about the choir. It was cold and flu season and the last thing she needed was to lose a few members the week before Christmas! "Is there a problem with the costumes?"

"Oh, nothing like that!" Candy assured her. "I told you, I have an in with the theatre. And Amelia is now giving the entire cast a closing night dinner on the house! All twenty-six actors, the director, the costume designer of course, not to mention the stage production hands..." She chewed her lip nervously; clearly, Amelia wasn't thrilled by the scale of this. "No, it's the carnival, dear. Gus pulled out his back and Cole is working on a big renovation in Pine Falls. I'm afraid we need all hands on deck if things are going to be set up in time."

The carnival started tomorrow, and it was well past dusk.

"We are part of the committee," Travis said.

She smiled at him. "And it is for a good cause."

And even though the cause wasn't directly solving her problem, the closer she got to Travis, the more she dared to think that her Christmas wish might just come true…and in more ways than one.

13

The Winter Carnival was an annual attraction for locals and tourists alike. Always hosted the weekend before Christmas, the entire town came out to participate in the games, eat the foods, and shop from the vendors who sold their seasonal items at the festively decorated kiosks.

Even a late night of hanging garland and counting out props for the children's game couldn't keep Jenna in bed much past daybreak. It wasn't like she'd slept much anyway. Between the anticipation of the children's choir performance and the memory of last night with Travis, her mind was too busy to rest.

She decided to stop off at the Buttercream Bakery for a coffee before heading over to the events, which would last through the weekend. As she walked past the town square, she saw that several vendors were already busy setting up their kiosks, and the decorations looked intact, even if many of them had been set up with only the glow from the Christmas lights and the moon to guide them last night.

Jenna was pleased to see that while it was busy as usual for this hour, Maddie was alone behind the counter, and there were at least four cranberry muffins left in the basket.

"Happy Carnival weekend!" Maddie grinned.

"What time are you closing up here?" Jenna asked, knowing that with so much of the activity centered around the carnival, most businesses that had stands closed up their shops for the weekend, leaving only the restaurants at the inns as dining options.

"My assistant already headed over to set up, but I wanted to oversee the morning rush. I heard from Candy that you were up pretty late last night setting things up—it was too bad Cole has that big job out in Pine Falls, because I know he would have loved to help." She sighed happily as she often did when she spoke of her boyfriend and then suddenly frowned. "My dad didn't climb any ladders, did he?"

Jenna laughed, even though it wasn't entirely funny. Her Uncle Dennis had fallen off a ladder and injured himself enough a couple of years back to warrant round-the-clock care. Of course, the fact that the aide had been Candy who ended up becoming his wife gave the whole story a much more positive slant in their family's memories.

"As if anyone would let him climb a ladder ever again!" Jenna gladly accepted the coffee that Maddie passed to her without being prompted, but her mind was back on last night, on the way her uncle and aunt and a few other townspeople had gotten the job done, working swiftly and efficiently. There hadn't been nearly enough time for talking. "No, Candy assigned all the climbing tasks to Travis."

"Oh." Maddie gave her a suggestive look that Jenna couldn't brush off if she tried.

Her cheeks flushed with heat when she said, "It wasn't like that. You know Candy…"

"I do. And I know you, too. And you, my dear cousin, are redder than the velvet bow on my Christmas wreath."

"Nothing happened," Jenna assured her, even though that wasn't true. Something had almost happened. She was sure of it. "We were all working on different things. I had to count out props and prizes for the children's games over at the town hall for most of the night. And Travis had to leave early to give his grandmother a ride home."

"Darn," Maddie said with a mischievous grin.

Darn was right. That had been admittedly disappointing, even though she wasn't sure what she'd expected. She lived in town, right in the center of Main Street. Did she want a snowy stroll down the quiet street with only the glow of the lampposts to guide their way?

With another flush, she realized that she had.

"Anyway, I'm just here for a cranberry muffin, and then I have to get to the carnival in case I'm needed."

Maddie selected the largest muffin from the basket. "Will Travis be in attendance?"

"He's part of the planning committee," Jenna said, trying to temper her anticipation. "And of course he wouldn't want his grandmother to miss it."

"Of course." Maddie handed her the paper bag with a knowing grin.

"And what can I look forward to tasting at your booth?" Jenna was desperate to get Maddie off the subject or idea of Travis. Her stepmother was wearing off on her, especially now that she was happily settled into her own relationship.

The question worked like a charm. Maddie's eyes sparkled and she nearly rubbed her hands together. "Individual plum puddings, traditional Victorian Christmas cakes, only for practical purposes, they will be cupcakes, and a chestnut dessert that was a little more of an undertaking than I had planned, though why am I not surprised since Candy never does anything on a small scale!"

No, she didn't, and in this instance, Jenna was grateful.

"Amelia is making mincemeat pies with *modern* ingredients, she keeps stressing. And Candy is making talmouse." Sensing further explanation was needed, Maddie said, "They're little pastries filled with cheese. You know how that woman loves cheese."

The whole town knew, but it had been her delicious cheese biscuits that earned her a spot in Amelia's kitchen where once only Maddie had been allowed to go.

"It all sounds so delicious that I'm not sure I should still eat this muffin!"

"You should and you will. Those are fresh from the oven ten minutes ago and the other three will be gone before you probably walk out the door."

It was true, and it made Jenna proud of her cousin's success. Most of her family members had found their way in this town, settled into careers they loved, and found someone special to share it all with, too.

"I should go and leave you to sell the rest, then." Jenna handed over the bill and left the change in the tip jar. Her cousin Heidi was coming through the door as Jenna opened it.

"I was just going over to the carnival if you wanted to join me?" Suddenly the thought of walking in alone made her feel too nervous, too obvious.

"Let me grab a latte," Heidi nodded.

Despite the cold, Jenna decided to wait outside rather than have two people teasing her about her personal life. She walked around the deck that ran the length of the building, facing the lake, which was partially iced over, the rocks that lined the shore were covered in a thick blanket of snow.

On days like this, she couldn't imagine that she'd ever hoped to leave this town.

"Ready!" Heidi came out holding up a steaming cup. "I know that they'll have plenty of treats at the carnival, but I thought I'd start with an adult beverage."

Jenna grinned. Heidi was also the youngest in her family and she was forever cast in the role of the baby, even though she was in her late twenties.

"There will be plenty of adult beverages," Jenna said as they walked. "Britt's doing wassail in addition to the cider and mulled wine."

"Wassail. Well, that sounds festive." Heidi stopped and said, "I almost forgot. Does this look old-fashioned enough for the theme?"

Jenna had already noticed that Heidi's usual hooded parka was replaced with a knee-length wool coat and a cashmere hat and gloves, all in what she knew Brooke would call "winter white."

"You look lovely," she said to Heidi, knowing that her cousin sometimes needed a little extra reassurance.

We all do, Jenna thought, thinking of her music.

"Lovely enough to catch the eye of a handsome gentleman?" Heidi laughed and sipped her latte. "I suppose it's probably too late to find romance this Christmas."

"Christmas is still a few days away," Jenna said, knowing that she was really holding out hope for herself, not just her cousin.

She finished her breakfast by the time they made it to the square, which was even busier than it had been when she'd first passed by it. As a child, Jenna loved the snowman decorating and sledding contests, but as an adult, she most loved walking the perimeter, sampling sweets from Amelia's and Maddie's booths, and feeling the Christmas spirit in the air.

This year, of course, would be extra special, and hopefully even more special for Mr. Pritchard.

"I'm not sure why I never thought of having the children perform before," she told Heidi.

"Probably because you were too focused on the school pageant to even consider a reason for doing something else. Sometimes you have to miss out on something to make room for something else. Of course, sometimes that often leaves room for *someone* else," Heidi said suggestively.

Jenna shook her head, but she couldn't deny that Heidi spoke the truth. Jenna had been forced to branch out, to try things she wouldn't have otherwise, much like all those years ago when her grand plan failed. She'd been left lost, uncertain of the path ahead, and somehow, she'd found another course. One that hadn't brought her fame or fortune, but had kept her right here in Blue Harbor.

Now, as children ran by her giggling, and couples walked hand in hand through the snowy festival, she couldn't imagine a year when she would miss this.

From a distance the church bells rang, prompting Heidi to glance at her watch. "Time slipped away. I'm supposed to be helping to set up the skating races. I'd better get going. See you later?"

Jenna nodded and watched as Heidi headed quickly toward the pond before deciding what she wanted to do next. The usual craft stands were a personal favorite of hers, and she often bought one of Mabel Gibney's knitted stockings or mitten sets as a gift, but this year she decided to wait on that and check on her family members first.

Cora's stand was always a favorite for locals and tourists alike, and she made sure to keep each year fresh, with ornaments that were unique and special. This year, Jenna couldn't help but smile at how perfectly she'd kept with the theme.

"It's straight out of the pages of a Dickens' novel," she said, admiring the old-fashioned ornaments that she almost didn't dare touch.

"It's an old-fashioned Christmas!" Natalie, who helped out in Cora's shop each winter when the big hotel on Evening Island closed for the season, lifted a particularly pretty glass ornament that was hand-painted with a snowy scene.

"It is," Jenna said wistfully. She looked around at the town square, which had been converted into a feeling of an old Christmas market. The games and sledding races and snowman building contest were well underway, but there were also roasted chestnuts, classic carols being played from the speakers, and even some people in costume, while others did the best they could with long wool coats and matching hats, forgoing the usual puffer coats that were admittedly more practical in northern Michigan.

"I should go find my carolers. This year we're taking shifts strolling the carnival."

"Be sure to come our way!" Cora was radiant as she finished setting up her stand, and Jenna promised she would as she turned to hurry to the town hall, where the Dickens-era costumes were waiting in their usual rehearsal space.

Travis was just coming into the park when Jenna hurried to leave it. At the sight of him, she felt a flush to her cheeks and her stomach rolled over, remembering the last time they'd seen each other and how they'd left things off.

Today, he was wearing a charcoal coat and a plaid scarf that had probably once belonged to his grandfather.

"I'm a little surprised to see you dressed for the theme," she admitted. She hadn't thought he'd go through with it.

"I'm full of surprises," he said, giving her a devilish grin.

She took a steadying breath and glanced away from those eyes, finding that despite the lake effect breeze, she was rather warm at the moment.

"Besides," he said. "My grandmother had a lot of fun with the idea. She had me rummaging through the attic for some of her old things. This included." He fingered the scarf. "I also came across a photo for that frame I bought her."

"Oh?"

"It's one of her and my grandfather, dated their first Christmas together. I'm guessing she either thought it was lost or forgot about it. It was mixed in with some old decorations that she said she hadn't put out in years. I'm hoping it will be a special gift."

Jenna shook her head, unable to fight her smile. "Why, Travis Dunne, I do believe you have a little Christmas spirit tucked away in there."

"I'm not a complete Scrooge," he said, his tone teasing.

"No," she said, letting her gaze linger on his handsome face, the trace of laugh lines around his eyes. "You're not."

He patted the scarf tied at his neck. "Well, it's an honor to wear something that was passed down through the generations. Made me stop and think what I would ever have to pass down." He frowned.

"I wish I'd thought to do the same at my parents' house," Jenna admitted. "However, Candy was able to talk a local theatre into donating their costumes to us for the next week, and I don't think anything I would have found could live up to that."

"I think you look fine just as you are." Travis's gaze trailed over her coat and back to her face, resting there. "Wonderful, really."

Her cheeks burned as she tried to fight off a smile. "Your grandmother isn't with you?" she asked, shifting topics.

"She's coming later. I thought I'd get an early start so I can see what this is all about before my shift at the children's events. Think they'll get a kick out of having their principal judge the snowman contest?"

She thought back on the way Keira had greeted him at the tree lighting and nodded. "You seem to have a real way with kids."

And his grandmother. And lately, with her.

She refrained from pointing out that it was a shame he didn't have the same influence with the school board.

"I guess it's because of how much the teachers and school experience meant to me growing up." He gave a modest shrug. "It feels good to give that back."

She couldn't agree more. "You haven't mentioned anything about the carols I selected to your grandmother?"

"Your secret is safe with me," he promised. He glanced over at the kiosks. "I don't know about you, but I'm starving. Can I buy you a bag of roasted chestnuts?"

"Oh." Jenna felt strangely disappointed at the thought of having to run off to carol, which was normally one of her favorite things to do all year, particularly because it usually only occurred once a year, on Christmas Eve. Today was a bonus, and one that she hadn't thought of before, and now suspected would be a part of every future Winter Carnival. "I'm about to run off and get in costume."

"I believe a top hat will be waiting for me at the judging table." Travis grinned.

"For once, your wool coat has a purpose here in Blue Harbor," Jenna bantered.

Travis laughed. "It may not be practical, but certainly suits the theme of the event. Will you stop by when you're finished?"

"Better than that, I'll make sure my group saves the best carol for when we walk your way."

"And I'll be saving you a cone of roasted chestnuts, if you're interested, that is?"

Jenna held her breath, realizing that the moment had come to admit to herself that she liked spending time with this man, and that she wasn't going to shy away from doing it more.

"It wouldn't be an old-fashioned Christmas without roasted chestnuts," she said with a grin.

"It's a date then," he said and walked away before she even had time to respond.

She turned, beaming, only to see Candy staring at her with wide eyes. "A date, is it?"

Jenna rolled her eyes. "A date, a time. A…" She couldn't exactly call it a meeting, which was the excuse she'd attributed to every other interaction she and Travis had over the last few weeks. The Winter Carnival was over, their professional ties would soon be over too, and any reason they had to spend time together after this would be strictly by choice.

*

Travis checked his watch and decided to explore the kiosks before heading over to the children's area to report for duty. He was already worried about playing favorites; he was all for healthy competition, but these were children, this was a festival, and well, it was Christmas.

And somehow, that had come to matter to him.

He chuckled to himself as he walked in the direction of the craft kiosks, where he'd helped his grandmother get set up when they first arrived, more than a little relieved to see the ruffle-edged baby blue scarf was being put up for sale rather than being wrapped and placed under the tree in the living room.

"Ah, Principal Dunne!"

Travis looked over to see May Rochet shuffling toward him. Like many of the locals, she had gotten into the spirit of the event and was wearing a long wool coat and a strange sort of bonnet.

"I barely recognized you," he told the chairperson of the school board. Even though they'd only met once, his first day on the job, he wasn't quick to forget such an influential face.

May patted her hat. "Too much?"

"Not at all," he said, laughing. "I have to say that I've never spent a Christmas quite like this. And I doubt I ever will again."

He frowned on that for a moment until she gave him a rueful look.

"Now don't go buying a return ticket just yet." May slid her eyes to both sides before stepping forward. "I probably shouldn't say this even though you'll know by Monday anyway, but Suzanne won't be returning."

She gave him a pointed look, one that didn't need explanation. "I have to say that the board has been pleased so far with what you've done. I think at Monday's meeting you'll find that many members, if not most, will be suggesting that you stay on here in Blue Harbor."

Stay in Blue Harbor? He hadn't thought it was a possibility; if anything, it had only started to feel like a dream. Or maybe, a wish.

A Christmas wish.

Travis blinked and pulled his chin back, letting her words sink in. "That's quite an endorsement."

"Well, you're quite a principal. The students have already warmed up to you and you have connections to the town."

"Roots," he said, catching himself. He'd never put down roots anywhere, never thought he had any, but patting his grandfather's scarf at his neck now, he knew that wasn't true. That he could stay in one place, grow a life, make memories.

The opportunity was being handed to him. If he wanted it.

And for maybe the first time ever, he knew exactly what he wanted.

*

Jenna hadn't expected the costume to be quite so itchy—or heavy—but it was surprisingly warm, especially given that she had been given the velvet blue dress while Candy stood out in crimson red.

"I think this is the best carnival we've ever had," Candy whispered in between songs. "In fact, I think caroling around the carnival should be made into a formal tradition."

Jenna couldn't disagree, and it would be nice to have some new rituals to look forward to, especially since the fate of next year's pageant was so uncertain.

She glanced at her watch, knowing that she could only put in a few more songs before she'd need to slip away to help assemble the children. Everything was riding on this. The crowd had come out, parents and board members would witness the beauty of the children's voices, and all she could hope for was that it swayed their minds about the fate of the music program. Or at least, softened their hearts.

"Let's do 'Deck the Halls' next," Candy announced, and seeing as no one quite belted out "Fa-la-la-la-la" like Candy, Jenna knew there was no room for argument.

They stopped every few feet, to sing directly to a family warming near one of the bonfires, or near the kiosks, where the crowds were already lined up for hot chocolate, spirits, or some of Maddie's fragrant baked goods.

The group knew each song by heart, of course, but still, it was more fitting with the style to hold a songbook, splayed in their palms. It was also a convenient excuse to hide her face when Candy got a little too enthusiastic.

Jenna noticed the brows of the passing Mr. Bradford shoot up when Candy hit a particularly high note. It wasn't enough that she was by far the loudest of her three fellow carolers. Her voice quivered on the note that she dragged out seconds longer than necessary, and there was a moment where every person at the nearby kiosks stopped what they were doing to stop and watch.

Jenna tried to flash her a look, but Candy didn't pick up on subtleties and instead used the encouragement to reach even higher in the next line. A crowd was now gathering, larger than the one even for the mulled wine, and Jenna flashed a glance over to the snowman building competition to see Travis staring at her from the judges' table, donned by a top hat and a rather handsome-looking scarf.

"I think that one was quite a hit," Candy announced afterward.

"It was something, all right," muttered poor Leonard Schultz, who had been with the choir for years, and who wasn't used to having his baritone overshadowed.

"I should get the children set up." A flutter of nerves went up inside her, and she was grateful when Candy clasped a hand on her wrist.

"They'll be wonderful. *You'll* be wonderful."

"How do you know that?" Jenna whispered.

Candy beamed. "Because you already are, honey. Don't let one person's opinion get you down. You just go and do what you do best. Bring music to those children and to this town."

Jenna knew that she should hurry, but she also knew that there was one thing more important to her than music, and that was her family. She pulled Candy in for a long hug, and Candy, loving hugs as she did, whooped with delight and swayed Jenna back and forth until they were both laughing.

"I'll be watching front and center!" Candy promised as Jenna pulled away.

Jenna was laughing as she hurried away toward the gazebo. There was no doubt about that, and she couldn't be more grateful.

As she helped the children to line up in their assigned positions, the crowd gathered around, and Jenna was relieved to see that Travis had made sure his grandmother and Mr. Pritchard were stationed in the front. She had considered making a small speech as a way to honor the man who had inspired her so much, but music spoke for itself, and with that, she raised her hands, the crowd fell quiet, and the children began to sing.

They sang all three songs without interruption, catastrophe, or accompaniment. This wasn't about her, this was about them, and she wanted their voices to float over the park until they sank into the hearts of every person in attendance.

When they reached the end of the final verse, Jenna gave them a broad smile, clasped her hands to her chest, and turned to face the crowd, who stood in silence for a moment before bursting into applause that lasted longer and louder than probably any other audience in the venues that she had once dreamed of performing in.

There was only one face in the audience that was not smiling, and that was Mr. Pritchard. Instead, tears streamed down his cheeks as she made her way over to him and clasped his hands in hers, noticing how warm they were, despite his lack of gloves.

"Thank you, my dear, thank you."

She smiled at him, holding back tears of her own. "No, thank you. I hope I made you proud."

"You have always made me proud, but this…seeing you carrying on my life's work, well, that is the greatest gift of all."

She gave him a firm squeeze, knowing that despite all the uncertainty right now, they had this moment. And it was perfect.

"Well, I don't know about you, but I could do with some of that wassail," Mabel said, giving Mr. Pritchard a suggestive glance.

"You two go on ahead," Jenna said, eyeing Travis as he stepped closer to her.

"That was very impressive," he said.

"Impressive enough to influence the board members? Or some of the parents to put pressure on them?"

"I hope so, Jenna. I really hope so." He stopped walking when they reached the row of stands. "I still owe you those chestnuts. I'm a man of my word."

A man of his word. Yes, she had started to see that this was true.

"I suppose I'm off the clock until my next round of caroling, but it will take a while to come down from all the anticipation." She looked around the snow-covered square; it was their best turnout that she could recall. "It looks like these past few weeks were a real success."

She looked up to feel Travis's eyes on hers. "I'll second that."

Jenna had the distinct impression that Travis was referring to more than their fundraising efforts.

"This has all been fun. Unexpected, but fun."

"Ah, so you *have* found your Christmas spirit!" She nudged him with her elbow, slipping on a hidden patch of ice in the process.

Travis grabbed her by the elbow, righting her, but he didn't drop his hand once she'd found her footing. She looked up at him, and higher, at the ball of greenery that hung down from the tree branch (Candy's touch—she'd scattered them all over and at random).

"It looks like we've encountered another holiday tradition." She nudged her chin until he followed her gaze. "Unless you haven't heard of that one either?"

His mouth curved into a slow smile. "I do know what mistletoe is, even if I haven't had the pleasure of experiencing it firsthand."

"This has been the Christmas for trying new things," she pointed out, well aware that both of his hands were still on her waist.

"And I have been enjoying all the Christmas activities," he said, pulling her a little closer. "And you do look awfully cute in this costume."

"Don't get too used to it," she warned.

He leaned down until his lips were almost brushing hers. "Oh, I intend to get very used to this. To this town. To Christmas. To you."

Jenna closed her eyes as her mouth met his, and despite the chill in the air, she'd never felt warmer, or more sure, that somehow, despite everything, this might just end up being the best Christmas ever.

14

By Tuesday morning, a fresh blanket of snow had covered the town square, erasing all evidence of the weekend's festivities, the sparkling Christmas tree returning to its position as the main attraction.

It was Christmas week, school was out of session, and Jenna was all too happy to give Keira an extra thirty minutes of lesson time so she could work on her song. It kept her mind from trailing to the thought of the board meeting, and what the outcome could be.

"That was wonderful!" Jenna told her, turning from the window. "I can tell you've been practicing."

"Only when my dad isn't home," Keira said, giving her a toothy grin. "It's going to be my Christmas present to him. I saved up my allowance to buy him a pair of Santa socks, but he told me he prefers homemade gifts."

Jenna managed not to laugh at the thought of Robbie Bradford in Santa socks. "Homemade gifts are the best. And of course, music is the greatest gift of all. I'm sure he'll love it."

"He'd better." Keira pushed back the bench and began gathering her music books. "I already spent my allowance money on a gift for Britt instead. Do you think she'll like Santa socks?"

"If they come from you, absolutely," Jenna said honestly. "Now what do you say we go get a treat from the bakery? Britt will pick you up there in half an hour." And after that, Jenna had accepted Travis's invitation to lunch, something that she'd been looking forward to ever since the carnival weekend had come to a close.

"Can I get the peppermint stick white chocolate cupcake?" Keira looked at her hopefully.

"We both can." Jenna winked, and they hurried to the hallway to grab their coats.

Jenna kept the conversation on Keira's wish list as they walked down the snow-covered sidewalks, but her mind was on the school, the board meeting that was taking place this week, and all that it meant for the music department. She told herself that regardless of the outcome, she'd tried her best. She reminded herself as she listened to Keira's happy chatter that she could still share her love for music with the children of this community, even if the school didn't support it. That next year, she could do another children's choir, one that she'd have time to prepare for, one that could rival the pageant that they might never have again.

Inside the bakery, the warm smell of chocolate greeted them, and Keira ran to the display case to study her options. Jenna wasn't surprised in the least that by the time they reached the front of the line, Keira had changed her mind and asked for an eggnog cupcake decorated like a snowman.

"Make that two," Jenna told her cousin.

"Hello, Keira!" Maddie carefully plated the treat so the frosting wasn't disrupted. "Have you finished your list for Santa?"

Keira nodded. "I have a few last-minute additions, though. You don't think it's too late?"

Maddie and Jenna exchanged a glance. "You should ask my sister that. Britt will be here soon, right?"

Jenna noticed a woman getting up from her table and motioned for Keira to grab it. "She's on her way. She told me the wassail was a big hit and that they might make it an annual holiday limited edition item."

"Some of my treats were well received too!" Maddie motioned to the chalkboard menu. "My Victorian Christmas cake cupcakes are available all week! A lot of good came out of the festival this year, and it didn't stop with the library fundraising."

No, Jenna thought, it didn't.

"And the look on your face confirms what I already know." Maddie waggled her eyebrows.

Jenna couldn't fight her smile, and she didn't want to, either. "You're just as bad as your stepmother, you know."

"Nothing wrong with wanting to see you happy." Maddie handed her the bakery bag. "Besides, you picked a pretty good guy from what I can see."

Jenna wasn't so sure that she'd picked him. More like, stumbled upon him, and in the most surprising way.

"I guess that good things sometimes come from tough situations," she said, thinking of how this related to other things in her life, too. How many times had she asked herself what her life might have become if she hadn't choked at her audition for the music college? It had set an entire chain of events into motion, and ultimately, one that had led her right to this moment, standing in the festive bakery, talking to one of her favorite cousins about a man who had just kissed her, at Christmastime nonetheless.

She'd almost say that this topped any New York City performance fantasy that she'd once entertained.

"Come join us when Britt arrives, although I can't stay long."

"Oh? More Christmas shopping, or something a little more…romantic?"

Jenna knew her expression would give the truth away. "I'm meeting Travis over at the Carriage House Inn for lunch. School's out on break, and I'm eager to hear how the board meeting went."

Maddie registered her anxiety and didn't tease her further about Travis. "Well, good luck. You know you have my support. And most people in town, too."

Jenna knew that now. She'd been silly to let Travis's offhanded comment ever shake her confidence about that.

She stepped aside to let the next customer place their order and made her way over to the table where Keira was making quick work of her cupcake, meaning Jenna would happily share hers. A gust of sharp wind cut through the otherwise warm room, and Jenna looked up in surprise when she saw who it was. "Suzanne? I thought you had to be down in Florida! Are you back for the holidays?"

Or, back to stay? Jenna had started to think that Travis might be more than a temporary part of town—and her

life—but seeing Suzanne here brought on a mix of emotions.

"I couldn't bear a Christmas without snow, and my mother has improved a lot these past few weeks. Enough for me to bring her back here for at least the holidays."

"So you'll be going back then?"

"My mother needs me, even though I can tell that I'm getting on her nerves. She says I fuss over her too much." Suzanne gave a guilty shrug and said to Maddie, "One of those delicious candy cane brownies, Maddie. Actually, on second thought, make that two."

"One for your mother?" Maddie asked brightly.

Suzanne's cheeks flushed. "Make that three, then."

Maddie gave Suzanne a wink and opened the display case, but Jenna still felt uneasy. These past few weeks had been so wonderful and she hadn't prepared herself for it to all come to a sudden end.

"Oh, look at me, being rude. How did the pageant go in my absence? I assume that you and Mr. Pritchard had it all under control as usual." She gave a fond smile.

Jenna stared at her. "There was no pageant. I thought you knew?"

Suzanne frowned. "Why ever not? You love the pageant! And it's Mr. Pritchard's final year!"

Jenna's heart was pounding as she stared at the woman, who looked every bit as confused as Jenna felt. If Suzanne didn't know about the pageant, that also meant that she'd had no intention of canceling it. And that maybe, she felt the same way about the music department.

"The music department doesn't have enough funding," Jenna said slowly. "It's at risk of being cut?" She tipped her head in question, looking for affirmation nearly as much as she hoped not to hear it.

Suzanne's mouth gaped. "I was aware that there was some pressure from the board regarding the budget, but I can assure you, Jenna, that before I left, I presented a plan to scale back on several smaller items that would have little to no impact on the curriculum as it stands. The board never pushed to cut the music program, specifically."

Jenna's mouth felt dry as everything started to form a clearer picture.

"Suzanne?" Maddie smiled at her from the counter and held up a bakery bag. "Your order is set."

"Oh, thank you!" Suzanne gushed as she rushed toward the bag. She took a long, deep smell and closed her eyes. "I couldn't imagine a Christmas without your candy cane brownies, Maddie."

Maddie's cheeks flushed with pride when she turned to the next customer, who placed the same order.

Jenna was still trying to make sense of this conversation. "I...I don't understand what's going on, Suzanne."

Only she did. And she had the sinking feeling that she had been right all along. That Travis Dunne was nothing but a Scrooge. A man without a heart. And that he had ruined a beloved Christmas tradition without any thought or remorse.

But then she thought of the man she'd come to know, the man who had baked cookies and built gingerbread houses, who had encouraged her to play the piano in front of a cheering crowd.

The man who had kissed her. The man who had made her realize what all the hype was about—not about Christmas. But about love.

She gave Suzanne a pleading look, hoping for some sort of explanation.

Suzanne looked torn as she slipped the bakery bag into her tote. She squeezed Jenna's arm and said, "We'll figure this out. Whoever thought that the music department and the Christmas pageant weren't worth fighting for isn't worth keeping around."

Jenna took no solace in Suzanne's passionate stance. The man that wasn't worth keeping around was Travis.

*

Jenna left Keira with Maddie and pushed out the door of the bakery. The slippery patches on the sidewalk didn't slow Jenna's pace any more than the lake effect wind made her feel the need to stop and button her coat. She hurried up to Main Street with a pounding heart, replaying her conversation at the bakery over and over, until there was no question or doubt left in her mind.

It wasn't all coming from the board. There had been one person standing between the pageant and the music program existing or not, and the decision rested with Travis.

Tears blurred her vision as she hurried across the street, but by the time she reached the door to the Carriage House Inn, she squared her shoulders and lifted her chin. This man wasn't worth crying over. The music department, her dreams, and the gift she'd wanted to give those children, that was worth crying over, but not now.

Travis was already seated at the bar, and he looked up and grinned at her when she approached, his expression folding to one of confusion when he saw the look on her face.

"Is something wrong?" He scanned her face for an explanation.

"You could say that. You could say a lot of things are wrong."

"Here, let me take your coat." He held out an arm but she took a step backward.

"I just talked with Suzanne. The former principal. I guess she's back in town for one last Christmas before she moves south to be near family. I suppose congratulations are in order. You earned a permanent position."

Travis's expression was unreadable. "I thought you'd be happy to hear that I was staying. I planned to tell you, today, in fact."

"And did you also tell me that you curried favor with the board by agreeing to their budget cuts, or rather, offering up a neat and tidy solution?"

Travis pulled in a breath and closed his eyes, confirming her suspicions and erasing any remaining doubt that she was holding onto. It wasn't until then, with her heart sinking into her stomach, that she realized just how much she had wished that this hadn't been true.

"I didn't decide anything, Jenna. The school's budget was a mess, and when I took over the position, I did the best I could with it. It would have been irresponsible of me to pretend there wasn't a problem."

"So you suggested cutting the pageant?"

He closed his eyes for a brief moment. "I viewed the pageant as an extra expense. The costumes, the props, all rented for a price that the school couldn't afford."

She almost didn't dare ask the most burning question, even though she already suspected the answer. "And did they decide to cut the music department next year?"

Travis didn't need to speak to give her an answer. The resignation in his eyes said everything.

"And let me guess, you were the one who suggested that, too?"

"When I first came, yes, but—"

She held up a hand. "You suggested it, and you clearly got your way."

He huffed out a breath in frustration. "Believe me, Jenna, if it could have been avoided, I would have found another way."

"I wish I could believe you, but I don't," she said, shaking her head. "When you believe in something, when you want something bad enough, you fight for it. Just like everyone fought for the library. I had hope, thinking that Suzanne was coming back... You gave me that hope."

"It was always possible that she would return. My position was temporary. Maybe Suzanne would have overturned things, or found a way."

"But you just said there wasn't a way," she pointed out.

She could tell by the silence that she had him there, that she was right, even when she'd never wanted more badly to be proven wrong.

"Look, I'm telling you the truth, Jenna. Maybe I was harsh at first, but I've gotten to know you, and I see how much you care. And I care, Jenna. I care about you."

"Funny way of showing it," she said, shaking her head.

"It wasn't personal, Jenna."

"Oh, it was very personal. To me. And this?" She pointed her finger at his chest and back at her own. "This isn't personal at all. And I shouldn't be surprised, because you've made a point of that, haven't you? Keeping everyone at arms' length, never getting too close?"

"Jenna, this isn't what I wanted."

"No, and what did you want?" She folded her arms across her chest and waited with a pounding heart to see if he would say something to undo all of this, to make it all different or better.

"That's just the thing, Jenna. I didn't know what I wanted. Maybe I never have. Maybe that's why I've bounced around so much, following in my mother's footsteps even though it had never made me happy. But here, I was happy. I found what I was looking for, and…I wanted to stay."

But staying meant on his terms, meaning no music department, no thought to what made her happy, or the children for that matter.

"It's too bad Suzanne didn't come back after all," she said angrily. "Not just for the school. But because this town doesn't need someone like you coming in and stealing its joy. Because you don't understand what that program meant to those kids. Or to me."

His eyes looked injured when she turned to walk away, but she told herself not to care. She couldn't care, not about someone who had broken her trust, and, somehow along the way, her heart too.

15

Christmas Eve Eve was apparently a thing, at least to Mabel Gibney. Whereas tomorrow night would be reserved for hot chocolate and the much-anticipated carolers that knocked on every door, tonight was for sitting by the tree and watching yet another holiday movie. Traditions came in all shapes and sizes, Travis was learning, but each one was special.

He crouched beside the fire and fed it another log. Behind him, his grandmother was sitting in her favorite chair, watching a movie that he now assumed she'd seen at least thirty times, given the way she kept saying the lines a few seconds before the actors.

But he wasn't paying attention, more like tuning it out. Jenna's words were sharp in his mind, and worse, they were true. But what he'd said was true, too. And now…well, now it was probably time to break the news to his grandmother before she heard it from someone else.

"There was a board meeting earlier this week," he said at the commercial break. "The last of the calendar year." He waited for her to ask a question, but she just looked at him in that patient way of hers, prompting him to continue. "They've offered me a full-time position. I guess they're happy with what I've done in my short time there."

She beamed, as he knew she would, and he braced himself for what he had to say next.

"Oh, of course they were happy with what you've done! Tell me, what do you think it was that cinched the deal? How great you are with the kids? And the staff?"

Travis huffed out a breath and studied the flickering flames. "I agreed to their budget cuts. I had an objective point of view, what I saw made sense, and...I wasn't emotionally invested." Until now. Now he saw things so much more clearly.

"Well, this is the best Christmas gift I have received since your mother was born." Gran's eyes misted slightly.

Travis looked at her, momentarily distracted. "You rarely mention her. I know you were disappointed she never visited."

"She didn't love Blue Harbor as I do. She wanted an adventure, and she was always chasing something bigger and more exciting. And I think she never quite got over your father breaking her heart," Gran added sadly.

Travis nodded. As he'd grown older, it was easier to understand the choices his mother had made, but somehow, however unintentionally, he'd always managed to follow in her footsteps.

"Those cookies you made, well, they were your mother's favorite. I haven't had them in years. Eating them again made me think of how much I miss her."

Travis swallowed the lump in his throat, letting the room fall silent for a moment. "I didn't mean to upset you."

"Oh, you didn't!" Gran said brightly. "It made me miss her, but it also made me remember all the good times we spent together, here in this house. Some people don't like holding on to the past, but I like to keep it alive."

"The thing is, Gran." Travis waited a moment before he hurt the one person he never intended to hurt. Other than Jenna. "I don't think I'm going to accept the position."

His grandmother frowned. "I'm not sure I follow."

"I don't agree with my initial position, and I think if I tell the board that, the offer will be rescinded." He looked at her squarely. "I've caused a lot of problems in a very short time. I think I should leave and let someone who knows the heart of this town take over the position instead."

"Nonsense! But you do know the heart of this town. If I didn't know better, I'd say you found your heart in this town, my boy."

He nodded slowly. He couldn't argue with her there. He'd found something special in this town. The possibility of love. The dream of a home. Maybe even the spirit of Christmas.

"I'm responsible for there not being a pageant this year. I didn't know how much it meant to the children, or Mr. Pritchard, or Jenna. I saw an easy way to scale things back, and I made a decision that looked good on paper. Unfortunately, the board agreed. And as part of that initial discussion, this will also be the final year for the school's music program."

There was a long pause before Gran finally spoke. "Oh, Travis."

"I know. I've let people down, people you care about, and...people I've come to care about." He reached out and took her hand. It felt thin and papery, but soft and warm. "I never meant to disappoint you."

Her eyes squinted into a smile as she reached out to pat his cheek. "Oh, my boy. The only thing you could do to disappoint me right now is to not take that job!"

He pulled back. Hadn't she heard a word he'd said? "But, Gran. I've done too much damage. I came in as outsider—"

"And now you're one of us." She gave him a knowing smile. "Moving all the time and running away from your problems is the easy way. Staying put and making things work, that takes courage."

"But, Gran." Travis shook his head. "I've ruined things for people here. I can't undo it, I tried." Oh, he'd tried suggesting they rethink the budget, but it had been too late, the solution was in place, so many problems had been solved that the board wouldn't even reconsider.

"Christmas is a time for hope," his grandmother said. "And sometimes even a miracle. If you want this to work, you'll find a way. You still have time to make everything right before Christmas, and wouldn't that be the greatest gift of all?"

Travis chewed his lip, imagining if such a thing were possible, but sitting here, looking at the twinkle in his grandmother's eye, he knew it was true just like he knew why she'd never left this town, even when she had no family left in it.

Blue Harbor had come together to save the library. And he was going to do everything he could to see that they saved the music department too.

*

As with every year, Christmas Eve seemed to come quietly and surprisingly, a bittersweet reminder that the season had passed quickly, but the best of it was still to come.

Jenna did not feel the same level of optimism this year.

Normally, after caroling, she'd head over to her childhood home, where she could warm her cold hands near the crackling fireplace, sip the hot chocolate that her mother kept on the stove, and nibble popcorn and cookies while watching *It's a Wonderful Life*.

Tonight, as she shuffled along with the rest of her group to the next house on Spruce Street, she could think of nothing better than going back to her apartment, changing into her flannel pajamas, and crawling into bed.

"Oh, not this one!" Leonard reminded them, giving them a look of warning.

Of course, this house had changed hands two years back, and the new owners had small children and hadn't appreciated the "noise" as they'd called it.

"A shame that not everyone has a Christmas spirit." Candy shook her head, but only after narrowing her eyes on the window of the small cottage.

Though most of Blue Harbor was accessible by foot or bicycle during the warmer months, the winter was unforgiving, and for that reason, the choir had broken out into five small groups, each covering a different part of town so that no house would be missed, unless specified.

Jenna's group consisted of Leonard, the Healys, who owned the farm next to Conway Orchard, and Candy, of course. Seeing as they were family, it only made sense, especially as all of their family member's homes were on their stops.

Jenna was looking forward to seeing a friendly face or two as they rounded the corner and began their way down Juniper Street, but she halted when the group started to make its way up an unexpected footpath.

"I don't think we should do this house," she said, remaining firmly on the sidewalk.

Leonard looked at her in confusion. "But Mabel loves our carols! She's never missed a year."

It was true, so very true, and as much as Jenna regretted the thought of disappointing Mabel, she couldn't bear the thought of facing her grandson. Tonight. Or ever again.

Luckily, since he'd played such a huge role in scrapping the Christmas pageant and music program, she probably never would.

"My throat is bothering me." She held a hand to her neck, her fingers skimming the lace collar that was part of the elaborate costume. "You guys go ahead. I'll join you at the next house."

She looked around for a place to hide, settling on the shadow of a large evergreen, where the moon wouldn't shine down and draw any attention to her.

"Nonsense!" Candy exclaimed. "We need you for our harmony!"

"Candy." Jenna looked at her pleadingly.

"*Jenna.*" If history proved anything, Candy wasn't going to back down on this, and Jenna sensed that she had better heed her aunt's insistence, even if she was technically in charge here.

Sighing deeply, she trudged back through the snow to her group, most of whom looked either confused or bewildered at what had just transpired, but Jenna knew that before they all dispersed tonight, Candy would be filling them in on every last detail—that was, if they didn't witness things for themselves.

Candy rang the doorbell and Jenna held her breath, wishing that she could hide behind her aunt's formative figure rather than stand shoulder to shoulder, as they'd practiced.

The door opened after a turning of the locks, and it took a moment for reality to catch up with her expectations. She stared at the blank space where she assumed Travis would be, her gaze eventually dropping to Mabel Gibney, who sat in her wheelchair, a plaid throw blanket on her lap, crimson lipstick on her mouth.

"Oh, I've been waiting for this all evening!"

Candy slid Jenna a look that didn't require explanation, and Jenna immediately felt guilty at almost disappointing this poor woman.

"We can wait until your grandson joins you!" Candy beamed, and now it was Jenna's turn to flash a look, one that Candy stubbornly refused to catch.

"Oh, I'm afraid he's not here," Mabel said.

Jenna and Candy both frowned. It was Candy who asked the question that Jenna was thinking: "He isn't with you on Christmas Eve?"

Mabel shook her head. "Had to leave. Something important came up, I'm afraid, and he had a change of plans."

A change of plans. Jenna chewed her lip, knowing that Travis never would have left his grandmother on Christmas Eve unless something very important had come up—he may not have much Christmas spirit of his own, but he certainly knew what the holiday meant to the woman sitting before her, shaking her head.

Could he have left town? Gone back to Florida, or moved on somewhere else so quickly? It was entirely possible.

"And you're all dolled up and all alone!" Candy, never one to refrain from stating the obvious, tutted.

"Oh, I'm not alone for long." Mabel gave a little smile.

So he hadn't left then. Jenna wasn't sure whether to be relieved or disappointed, and it troubled her that she was even remotely conflicted. Her heart picked up speed as she darted her eyes to the driveway. There were fresh tire tracks in the snow. Maybe Travis had left to run an errand. Maybe he needed to pick up something from the grocery store before it closed until the day after Christmas. That would classify as important. That would warrant leaving his grandmother on Christmas Eve.

"Mr. Pritchard is picking me up shortly. I was so afraid I would miss you all!"

Not Travis then. Jenna glanced at her group. "Well, shall we begin then?"

They sang Mabel's favorite—something they did with all the homes they visited over the years. Some they knew from requests, others from the sheer joy that came into their neighbors' faces. Sometimes, like Mabel, it was the tears in her eyes. Not from sadness, Jenna knew, but from a memory.

"My husband loved that song," Mabel said wistfully once they were finished. "It's funny how even when people have been gone for years, somehow, especially at Christmas, it's like they're still a part of you. Thank you, all of you." She held Jenna's gaze the longest. "Thank you, Jenna. You're a very special young woman."

Jenna swallowed back the knot in her throat.

"Have a wonderful Christmas, Mrs. Gibney," she said, backing away. No one in the group spoke again until they'd reached the end of the driveway and began moving toward the next house.

"See? Travis wasn't even home," Candy said with a wink as she linked Jenna's arm.

Jenna wasn't sure what to make of that, or why her chest felt so heavy. It was Christmas Eve, her favorite night of the year, and she was caroling, with people who shared her love for music, even if some of them, like Candy, perhaps enjoyed it a little too much.

"Who's next on the list?" Jenna asked.

"Just these two homes here and then it's back into town. A few people are gathering over near the library. I think the mayor is going to announce that the library has been saved. Wouldn't that be a wonderful Christmas gift to the town?"

"Imagine that," Jenna let out a breath, but she was smiling for all the work they'd done, and the thought of life in Blue Harbor being able to continue as it always had, even though change was inevitable, even in their small little part of the world.

And just like all the times before, she tried to find hope in her latest setbacks, but right now, she was struggling, even though it was Christmas.

*

By the time their small group arrived at the library, shivering and eager to warm their hands and maybe soon indulge in a hot beverage, a large crowd had already formed.

"This is quite a turn-out!" Jenna said. "But I guess it's for a worthy cause."

"Oh, very worthy," Candy said with a little smile as she hurried over to her husband.

Jenna was only mildly surprised to see her parents standing beside Uncle Dennis, and she waved to get their attention, but Candy had already made her way to them and was already deep in conversation.

Jenna looked through the thick crowd for her sisters or cousins, but instead, she saw Mr. Pritchard. Her heart sank a little when she considered that this wouldn't just be his final year, but the final year for the department. It was bittersweet in many ways; the program would always have his mark on it. She couldn't walk away without saying hello.

"Oh! And Mabel!" She looked in surprise at the woman sitting in the chair beside him. "We meet again. I suppose you're here for the mayor's announcement before you get on with your special plans?"

"I'm here for the best Christmas gift of all," Mabel said with a wink and patted Mr. Pritchard's hand as he helped her to stand.

Jenna looked at her quizzically but shrugged it off. Mabel Gibney had always loved the community here in Blue Harbor; it should come as no surprise now that she was finding personal joy in seeing the town's traditions preserved.

"I heard about the board's decision." Jenna willed herself not to cry as she looked into Mr. Pritchard's kind blue eyes.

"It's okay, my dear. I had a good run. The best really."

Truer words were never spoken, and Jenna swallowed back her emotions as she turned away from the two lovebirds, happy to see Helena was within arm's reach.

"Oh, Helena! What a turnout!"

"I know!" Helena's eyes sparkled. "I probably say this every year, but I have to say that this has been the best Christmas ever!"

Jenna pushed back the hurt in her chest and managed a smile for her friend, wishing she could say the same for herself.

"It's funny how sometimes when it feels like all is lost that you realize just how much you found." Helena squeezed Jenna's hand, but when her eyes looked over her shoulder, her expression changed. "Oh! There's the mayor now!"

Sure enough, Mayor Hudson was moving through the hallway, greeting the members of the town as he walked, stopping momentarily to grin in Helena's direction.

"Are we ready?" he asked, and Helena nodded.

"So you already knew?" Jenna supposed that she would have had to, considering the entire town was gathered in a building that was typically closed by this time of night on Christmas Eve.

Helena couldn't stop smiling as she released Jenna's hand and walked toward the solid oak double doors that housed the children's section and pulled the knobs, revealing a crowded space of faces that Jenna recognized, even though she could barely process what she was seeing. There were Britt and Robbie, and her cousin Natalie, and the Jacobs and the Millers and all the other families of the children she taught…and not just for piano lessons. These were the parents from the school. And there, at the very back of the room, were the children, lined in rows by grade level, the smallest at the front, all in costume, from the angels to the elves.

"It's your Christmas pageant, my dear."

Jenna turned to see Mr. Pritchard standing beside her as hot tears welled in her eyes. "But…I don't understand."

"It wouldn't be Christmas in Blue Harbor without this pageant. The very same one we do each year. And will continue to do, every year."

"Oh, Mr. Pritchard." Jenna blinked quickly, trying to make sense of what he was saying. She felt every eye in the room on her, even as the rest of the crowd shuffled quietly to find a seat. "But I wanted to give you a concert. I wanted that to be my gift to you."

"Oh, Jenna. Giving is the greatest gift of all. And you've given these children the same love for music that I was honored enough to share with you. I'm so proud of you, Jenna. And I hope. Well." He glanced over her shoulder. "I think Principal Dunne can take it from here."

"Principal..." Jenna started, but not before Travis stepped around in front of her, his expression somber, but his eyes hopeful. "I don't understand, Travis. I thought you left town. Your grandmother said you had something important to do."

His mouth crooked into a smile. "Something very important. I had a Christmas wish to fulfill."

"You mean you did this? All of this?" She looked around the room, at all the happy faces, at the joy and expectation in the children.

"Oh, I had help. From Mr. Pritchard. And my grandmother. And the mayor. And Candy, who helped secure the costumes. And Helena, of course."

From the doorway, Helena winked.

"I talked to the mayor. I explained the situation with the school's budget and he decided to allocate some of the proceeds from this library fund to the music department. There's more than enough, and that's mostly on account of you. And everyone here. I didn't know if anything would come from it, but I had to try, Jenna, because like you said, when you want something bad enough, you fight for it. And I...I want you, Jenna."

She swallowed hard. "Travis."

"I know what I said, and I know what I've done, but I meant it, Jenna, when I said that I didn't know you when I put all this into motion. I didn't know the town, or the people, or what the music department meant to them. But I know what it means now. And I want to be a part of it. I want to be a part of this town. And I want to be a part of your life."

"You don't like to stay in one place for long," she reminded him.

His mouth crooked into a smile. "That's because I never found a home before now."

"Or Christmas," she said, feeling her heart lift as she smiled up at him. "So the music department is saved?"

"On one condition." Travis lifted his eyebrows. "The school will need a new music teacher. That is if you're open to it."

"Open to it?" She laughed through her tears. "I couldn't think of anything better. I couldn't think of anywhere else I'd rather be."

And it was true, she realized, standing there, in the building that was as familiar to her as her own home, surrounded by her family, her friends, people who had known her since she was a little girl, and one in particular whom she had only just met but was very eager to know better. And longer. Maybe even forever.

Travis took her hands in his. "Me either, except maybe under a sprig of mistletoe."

She grinned up at him. "I'm willing to forego tradition this once if you are."

"Let's call it the start of a new tradition," he said, leaning down to kiss her, slowly, sweetly, with absolutely no mistletoe required, only the sound of music as the children started to sing, and maybe, just maybe, a touch of Christmas magic.

ABOUT THE AUTHOR

Olivia Miles is a *USA Today* bestselling author of feel-good women's fiction with a romantic twist. She has frequently been ranked as an Amazon Top 100 author, and her books have appeared on several bestseller lists, including Amazon charts, BookScan, and USA Today. Treasured by readers across the globe, Olivia's heartwarming stories have been translated into German, French, and Hungarian, with editions in Australia in the United Kingdom.

Olivia lives on the shore of Lake Michigan with her family.

Visit www.OliviaMilesBooks.com for more.

Made in the USA
Coppell, TX
05 November 2021

65233781R00129